DANIEL DORE

The Red Widow Group

Contents

1

Chapter 1

THE GOLDEN DONDERI SAGA
  THE RED WIDOW GROUP
  A Novel by
  Daniel Dore
  ddorebooks.com

Alone at last. I thought he would never leave for his stupid board meeting. Hopefully he will have to leave for a long trip to some other world and the swelling on my face will come down enough that I could cover it up with makeup and eat out at a restaurant or something. He might be one of the richest men in all the systems, but I would settle for a modest man with barely enough money to live by if it meant he would love me and treat me right. But I can't leave Alan as he has a clause that if I leave him, I get nothing for the six years of marriage and find myself on the streets and pray to anyone out there who will get their hands on me.

So, I bid my time and hope that I will survive long enough

to get the one million credits promised me if we are married more than fifteen years. Only nine years to go of getting beaten up regularly and sex that feels more like rape then love.

I slowly get out of bed, the pain in my back just shy of crippling, and put on a day gown. I walk to the stairs and make my way as best I can down to the lower level of the Penthouse Alan owns over one of his numerous OK. I haven't been out of this apartment ever since arriving after our wedding, a heartless affair in front of his family and friends, where all of them looked at me like a piece of meat. Some of the male guests actually came up to Alan and asked him when they could have their turn on me. His answer should have rung sirens in my head as he told them 'not yet'. He didn't say never, just not yet.

Well since then a few of them had their turn with me and they were even worse than Alan. I can only imagine their wives and the torture they are getting right now. Some days I'm not even sure I'll survive the night, but I always seem to pull through and, in the morning, Alan almost looks disappointed when I get up from bed to take a shower.

I'd probably leave even if it meant being broke, but Alan has the place watched twenty-four seven, the old Earth term for all the time. In the kitchen I find the trusted and always present Gregory Hick. Personal Aid to my husband, he is always by my side whenever Alan needs to leave for extended periods. A small smile crosses my lips but I wipe it off just as fast before he sees it. Alan might think himself clever, 'giving' me a shoulder to cry on, but I quickly found out that Greg reports every single word I usher to him right back to Alan.

I walk up to the food dispenser and ask for an herbal tea, no sugar, take the cup and slowly walk to the table to read the news on my tablet. After a few redacted pages I switch to the out of system news, see what I can find out about the Alliance that I might learn that hasn't been blocked.

Alan gave me the tablet the next day after the wedding and I had the 'nerve' to ask him why I couldn't read about a certain system where my parents lived. That day was my first beating. He told me that I read what he wants me to read, I eat and drink what he wants me to eat and drink, and if I gained an ounce of fat I would get beaten until I lost it and then some more for me to remember the lesson. That day when he left for work, I tried to slip away but came face to face with Gregory Hick. He showed up with a smile on his face and a shoulder to cry on. It took me four months to put together that he was Alan's favorite dog and reported back everything I said back to him. Since then, I have kept my comments to a minimum.

Greg sees that I'm not in a talking mood and he simply heads to his office closing the door. No doubt he'll be watching me on his numerous monitors all day long. I can feel his eyes when I go to the bathroom, when I eat at the table, and even when I take my shower, no doubt tossing off at the same time. He's never asked Alan for his turn with me but I'm sure he's got permission to please himself while watching me. Knowing Alan, it's probably written in his contract.

I head back to the room and give Greg his daily pleasure before crawling back in bed and sleeping the pain away for a bit.

* * *

The most beautiful scenery stands before me, with dozens of different kinds of flowers all spread in swaying patterns that attract the eyes and bring a smile to your face. No one else

3

around stares at the flower beds, but all have the same smile I do. I walk a few steps toward the closest flowers and stop suddenly, noticing that I have a flowing gown of spun gold that envelops my body to leave nothing to the imagination. The perfection of it even surprises me, but I notice something I haven't noticed in a long time, the absence of pain.

I slowly bend down to the soft petals and lose myself in their incredible smell. Suddenly a warning tickles my brain and I swirl around faster than I ever did and push my hand toward a trio of very large men walking toward me. The men go flying backwards hitting a few people in the process.

All around people run away screaming and a little farther away, too far to help for now, the city guardsmen are running in this direction. They will never get here in time to save me, why I know this is beyond me. A burning feeling inside me rages through my veins and all of a sudden, my vision turns red and I can feel power like nothing anyone has ever felt. The three men are back on their feet and spreading out to surround me, but it won't matter anymore, as the power has awakened inside me and there is nothing these Vuldalian soldiers can do to stop what's coming their way.

The power forms inside me, guiding me to the best way to get rid of the threat and I spread my fingers wide at the same time as I spread my arms wide. I instruct the power to take out all Vuldalian assassins in the area. Believing the power would spread into three rays of power, I'm as surprised as everyone else when seven rays extend from my fingers and not only do they find the three soldiers in front of me, but also a sniper in the trees across the garden and three other assassins hidden in Conranian clothing.

As the rays stop and the after effect of the bright light in my eyes diminishes, all that is left of the enemy soldiers is ash. Even the body armor they had been wearing is gone. I expect everyone around to keep screaming and running away but all come back and a few walk up to me asking if I am OK. Others walk to the ashes and simply brush them aside with their boots, as you would dirt or garbage.

And then one person asks something I never would have thought to hear.

"Princess, how's the baby taking the power surge?"

* * *

I wake with a start, breathing hard as if I had just been in an incredible battle instead of sleeping in bed. Steps outside the door announces the coming of Gregory. I already know what he's gonna ask before he even opens the door.

"Nightmare my lady?" he asks, making the question sound disgusting instead of respectful.

"Yes Greg. Nothing new."

As he leaves the room, I know nothing about the dream had been normal, or old news. I've never had anything like it in my life, so real you believe you're actually there.

Princess? A baby? If anything, I was far from a Princess and definitely not pregnant, Alan made sure of that. But it was still clear in my head, as if I was that person in my dream. Something about the dream made it impossible. Conranian. The me in the dream had said the assassins had been dressed with Conranian clothing to blend in, so that must have been on Conra V, the mythical planet where the supposed super beings lived in the far past. The stories went on that they had been eliminated by a race called Vuldalian, bred to eliminate

5

threats like the Conranians.

This was back a few centuries if the stories were even true. So, it was impossible the person in my dream would have been me. Could it have simply be a normal dream and it just felt like it was real? But something in it felt real, not just the woman but the whole surroundings. Even though I've never set foot on Conra V, it has been destroyed for a few hundred years, I could recognize several of the items I could see in the dream. I slowly get up from bed and grab a night gown even though it's still morning. Before I can put it on Gregory's hurried steps come walking to my door. No knock or anything, he storms into the room screaming.

"How did you do it bitch?"

The level of hatred in his voice tells me something bad has happen, and of course it's my fault.

"What are you talking about Greg?" I barely get out of bed before he slaps me across the cheek.

"Who did you hire? You're going to answer me bitch or I'll slap you until you die."

He slaps me again on the other cheek. The force is almost as hard as when Alan slaps me. I can hear several more footsteps coming up the hall toward the room, one of which is heels. Greg goes to slap me again but a large voice stops him.

"Sir! The Master has forbidden you from hitting her too hard. I will have to report this."

"Report it to who Jansen. The boss is dead. His ship just exploded before jumping out of the system. No one saw any pods escaping. That bitch did it somehow, and I intend to find out how."

Both huge bodyguards turn fire filled eyes toward me, and I know my time has come. Suddenly something builds inside me, the same feeling I felt in the dream. As if the dream was telling me I would need this power, the energy filled every pore in my body and sparks start to fly between my fingers. I don't wait for them to move another step and spread my hands open to release three spears of lightning strong electricity. All three men are stopped and a split second of fear appears in their eyes before they burn to ash and the power leaves my hands back to normal, but doesn't leave me altogether like it did in the dream. Seems more enemies might be nearby. I remember the heels and look toward the door to find Geraldine Cameron, Alan's accountant and I believe my only friend in his empire.

Geraldine approaches slowly and looks at the three ash piles on the marble floor, then at me, also with fear in her eyes. She has something else in there as well, but I can't explain what it is I see.

"Sherry-Ann, are you OK?" she asks.

"Not sure how to answer that. First, is the news about Alan true? He's really dead?"

"He is, I made sure of that. I knew something was up last month when he hired those two mountains by the door. I dug deeper without him knowing and found that he had taken a blood sample from you and had it tested. Something about how fast you healed made him nervous. I found the blood results in an email he sent a group of crazy people that call themselves the Cleansers. They are a race called Vuldalian and are only after one race, Conranian. I checked the blood sample again and found you were of that race. The two goons were to come in and kill you as soon as Alan was out of the system, preventing anyone from accusing him. I made sure his ship would blow up before he made it to jump."

"But those two did come in to kill me, so your plan failed."

"Well, I stormed onto the floor as soon as I got confirmation of the ship explosion and that no survivors had been found, but Greg was faster than I was. I had already brought something to surprise the two out there."

She pulls a blaster out of her handbag. Somehow, I knew it would not have done much against them.

"Well, now you don't have to do anything to them. What now? I'm pretty sure more of his goons are closing in on the penthouse to finish what Greg wanted to do. Alan had thousands of men at his disposal."

"He did. Not anymore. Now all of it is yours."

2

Chapter 2

"Geraldine, what are you talking about? Alan would never leave me anything. Hell, in the back of my mind I was even wondering if he would have me killed right before our contract came up just to save some money."

"That's exactly what he was gonna do, and that's only if you lasted that long. All Alan ever cared about was money, nothing else."

"Then why would he leave me anything at all, let alone everything?"

"Because I tricked him into doing it."

"I don't understand."

"Alan is overcautious about his assets, so I had to be creative. When I learned who or what you are, I knew the time had come to put it in action. I created a program that copies the opened document in style and form, but with the information I wrote on it. I wrote up a will placing you as his only receiver of everything he had at the time, making all wills before that one void. Since Alan was always paranoid, he changed his signature every week and sent a copy to it to his bank to make sure no one could use an old one to forge a document. So, I had to make sure the plan would happen before the week was over.

My half-brother, one Alan knew nothing about, was hired several years ago to work on his ships as a mechanic. He happens to be an ex-military special ops explosive expert, hates women beaters, and was able to rig the primary ship Alan used to blow up just before jump. All he had to do was enter a series of numbers that no one would see as other than diagnostic requests. The second I knew he was going off on one of his trips I activated the plan. As I knew Alan was leaving today, I had him sign some documents yesterday and made sure my best friend, a drop-dead gorgeous woman, was assisting me in filing some physical documents, and that she would bend over at just the right moments so that Alan would be too busy looking at her ass and cleavage to pay attention to anything he was signing.

Just before he left my office and was gonna ask my friend to join him, I reminded him that he had a meeting a few minutes later with the planetary President so all he ended up doing was slap her ass. Katherine was glad to take the slap for you as she was once in the same shoes, with a man that treated her like trash. I sent the real document as well as the will at the bank for certification and then set everything else in motion. Now you own everything."

I stand silent for a moment before remembering that other people will be here soon to see what has happened in the room, or to check up on what's really going on with Alan. I need a game plan for the immediate future if for no other reason than to survive long enough for the information about me owning everything comes out. After that we can see. Something

Geraldine said comes back to mind and it gives me an idea.

"Well, if I own everything my first order of business is to hire you as my personal aid and accountant, with a much-needed raise I might add. Not sure how much you make but for now just double your salary and we can go from there and adjust up later. Second, I need personal security. Your half-brother looking for a new job? I find myself in need of someone I can trust to lead a new security force."

"Well thank you boss. I'll give Brad a call right away. I'm sure he'd love nothing better than working for you."

"Good. Oh, also ask him if he has similarly minded ex-military buddies also looking for a job. Men or women are welcome, as long as they are all on the same page."

"Do you have a plan already boss on what you want to do with your new found fortune?"

"Not quite yet, but I have a feeling we're gonna make a lot of enemies really mad in a very short period of time, and having a good security force surrounding us might be a good strategy."

Geraldine nods and grabs her comm to call Brad. I'm not sure how many of Alan's business buddies really liked him, but with the amount of money he helped them make, the number could be very high, all with literal armies at their disposal. I walk to Greg's desk and scroll through the security screens still open. I was right, he could see me in the shower and I will definitely need to clean this desk off before anyone works on it. No one else seems to be inside the penthouse besides Geraldine and I, but when the first elevator screen comes on it shows several very large men in the same uniform as the two large guards that came in my room. I'm not sure I can replicate what I did earlier but I might have to if we're going to survive the next few minutes.

11

Geraldine walks fast toward the desk with a bit of fear in her eyes. She's probably heard the elevator doors open and the numerous booths hitting the ground coming toward us.

"I can't reach Brad and his boss told me he left his shift early and has not been seen since. I hope Alan's goons haven't figured out he's the one who rigged the ship to blow. Oh God what have I done?"

"Geraldine, relax. Now's not the time to come apart. We have a more pressing problem to handle first."

I nod toward the entrance doors and soon five men, no make that five mountains barely fit in the door jam and purposefully walk into the penthouse. All are armed for war and the leader's face could probably break rocks just looking at them. Let's see if I can make a convincing CEO. I get up from the desk and walk closer to them, confidence I don't feel showing in my walk and gestures.

"Can I help you gentlemen somehow?"

"You the bitch wife we're here to kill?"

"Well now, that's no way to talk to a lady who could have you thrown into the nearest sun just by glancing at the planetary President. Actually, it's not the way to talk to any lady at all."

"Same old Conranian superiority complex. You people think you're better than anyone else, yet we managed to almost eradicate your race with a smaller force and bigger wits."

"Better wits might be a better choice of words, but then again I wouldn't expect the likes of you to actually be able to think. Heck, your combined IQ is probably smaller than my late husband's dick. And let me reassure you, that is a pretty low number."

"Why you stinking bitch…"

The leader never got to finish his sentence as the two rear

12

men went down fast and hard soon followed by the next two. Before the leader could even move to see what was going on, he had one of the largest knives I've ever seen placed directly under his chin. One move and he would lose his head. Six men and women come walking in behind the very large man holding the knife. Large and very dashing I might add. The man turns his head toward me and barely nods, his eyes never leaving the mountain.

"Morning boss, sorry we're late. Had to take the stairs on the account that five idiots took the only elevator up here. Sis."

"No problem at all Brad. I believe there is a garbage shoot off to the right of the elevator that goes directly to the basement of the building. Might be the best place to throw this garbage out."

"I like your style boss. Garbage shoot it is. Men?"

While Brad kept the leader held under the threat of his knife, the rest of his team took the other four and threw them away the only way they deserved. Then the team joined their leader and surrounded the mountain and stared at him with eyes that rivaled even his earlier stare. Brad turned the guy's head toward him with pressure from his knife and looked him in the eyes.

"Alive or dead pal, your choice. One way or another you're going down that shoot."

The mountain slowly turned and Brad followed his movements, his knife never leaving his neck. A few minutes later the seven ex-soldiers walk back in the apartment, all business in their movements. Brad motions for two to guard the door and the other four to scout the apartment and make sure it's safe. Brad walks up to me and his sister giving her a smile before turning toward me.

13

"My people will make sure your safe from now on boss, if you'll have us?"

"Brad, the minute you seven walked into that stairwell you became employees. Not sure what salary you normally make for this type of work, but Geraldine will fill me in on some of the details. Hell, I'm not sure how much I have and what I own."

"I'm not sure we have time to talk about that right now." Says my new accountant.

At that moment the four searching the apartment come back and give Brad a nod, probably signaling the all clear.

"I want one at the elevator and two at the door, rotation every hour for now. Get the gear out and prepare for war." Brad tells his team.

The six men and women walk out of the apartment and come back a few seconds later with bags full and heavy. All are open and all sorts of weaponry are taken out, an assault rifle taken to Brad as well as a large hand blaster.

"Unless they plan on blowing the whole building to pieces, you have plenty of time to talk business ladies."

Brad nods again and goes to walk away.

"Brad, I'd like for you to stay please." I say.

"Boss? I'm not sure it's a good idea for a security officer to know how much his boss has."

"And why would that be?"

"Well, he might try to get more money out of him or her."

"Well, this might be strange to say, but I believe the contrary. For the last few minutes more and more thoughts have popped into my head, like going to school but on super-fast forward. This could be a result of the Conranian power now flooding through my veins, but I am thankful for them anyway. I don't really care how much credits I have, but my belief is that all my employees should profit from this money, instead of it just accumulate in the banks and serve no one. I want at the very least my accountant and my security chief to understand the amount of danger that might come their way because of the amount of money I have."

"Told you she was bright." Geraldine tells Brad.

I blush a little but I have to move on otherwise Brad will notice my eyes linger a bit too long on him.

"So, Geraldine, how much do I actually have?"

"Well, that difficult to say right of the bat. A lot of assets might be forcefully taken over by rival companies, you also have a lot of cargo coming and going through the shipping companies, and a hundred different things like that."

"You make it sounds like I own a dozen companies or something." I say.

"Actually Sherry-Ann, you own four hundred thirty-four companies."

Brad's reflexes are good as he steadies me just as my knees are about to give way. I steady myself and touch his hand.

"Thanks." I tell him.

"Don't mention it Boss."

"Sherry-Ann please Brad, no more of this Boss thing. That goes for all your men as well. Boss seems so formal, and I am nothing like that. Now, without giving me a precise number, what are we talking about amount wise?"

"Well, in pure credits in the banks, you have a little more than fifteen trillion credits. The approximate value of the companies combine would more than triple that. And then add another few hundred billion credits for all the ships you own."

This time I'm able to stay on my feet but barely. I can even see Brad's eyes looking at me to make sure I don't fall over.

"Wow. I know I should be shouting the word out, but I'm not sure what to do with all that money. Geraldine, are you able to write up contracts for yourself as well as for my new security team?"

"I can do that right now if you want me to."

"Please do so. I know we'll need to move fast, but I want to be sure that the core of my new organization is stable. Brad, do you have other ex-military people that you could trust?"

Geraldine moves off and takes out her computer to start working.

"Well, I might have a few that I could trust, but most were pigs that would more likely whistle at the women soldiers than fight the enemy."

"Alright, get in touch with the ones you know will be respectful. Also, I need you to start recruiting good people. I don't care from what background they come from. All I care about are their manners toward other humans or others."

"Even criminals Sherry-Ann?"

"If a man robbed a bank so he could feed his family, should he deserve to spend the rest of his days in prison while people like Alan become extremely rich and screw people of their savings? I trust you to make the right call. Do you have someone in your team that excels in computers and data scrolling?"

"I'll start recruitment myself right away. Diana Gnalls would be your best bet for anything data. I'll have her come see you."

"Thanks Brad"

I walk to Geraldine and soon see that she's probably prepared some of this in advance hoping her plan would work. All of the contracts are ready except for one very important item.

"Hey Sherry-Ann, all I need now are the salaries for everyone."

"Alright, let's start with yours. What was Alan paying you?"

"Sixty-four thousand a year."

"And you looked after all his financials, right?"

"Yes."

"Well, that's just plain crazy. Please change that to two hundred a year for now. We'll adjust higher as the workload goes up."

Her eyes almost pop out of her head from the salary I give her, but thinking of an accountant controlling trillions of credits only making sixty-four thousand a year is ludicrous. Hell, she should be making at least a million, but seeing her reaction makes me happy I didn't suggest it right away. All in good time.

After coming over her shock of her raise, she pulls out the contracts for the seven soldiers now working for her. I have no idea how much personal security teams make, and I know anything Geraldine would give me would be based on what Alan paid his people, so grossly under what it should be. I need an expert in the matter. The good thing is he happens to be walking with a young woman my way.

"Sherry-Ann, this is Diana Gnalls."

To my surprise, Diana is Kroh. The Kroh are an intelligent race, adept of the electronics and technology. Most of their race study in these fields and are paid well for it. A peaceful race, it is rare to see one on a warship, so it's surprising to see Diana as a soldier.

Just as the information has been popping into my head on leadership and other topics, the language of the Kroh also comes to me. I will need to find someone that knows about my race to understand this process. I address Diana in her native tongue.

"I bid greetings to you and wish you safety and health."

Both Geraldine and Brad have not understood a thing I said, but a smile crosses Diana's lips, which is a rare thing for her race. They rarely show emotion except in the safety of their own.

"And I to you as well." She replies in her language as well.

"I have no clue how I know your language or your history but I do and want to thank you for coming to my rescue by paying you the respect of talking to you in your native language."

She answers in English.

"I thank you for the honor Sherry-Ann, but for the benefit of the others, would you be dishonored if we talked in English?"

"Not at all Wise Woman. I would require your help in finding information on all the ships it seems I own. I need to know their types, capabilities, and crew. I will also need to know how trustworthy each crew member can be to me. Basically, I need to get rid of all idiots that cannot follow a woman and will be disrespectful towards not only me but to others as well."

"And how soon would you need this information Great One?"

I smile at this as most Humans, Geraldine and Brad included, would think Diana is being disrespectful and sarcastic by her comment, but that is actually how most of the Kroh called the Conranians, and most of the Conranians called the Kroh either Wise Woman or Wise Man. She was just thanking me for the use of her official title in the old Empire.

"Within the hour would be perfect."

Again, both Humans thought that bad blood might be

brewing between the two women, but nothing was further than the truth. Giving a Kroh an unreasonable time frame is a mark of honor, showing that I consider her skills to be better than they might be.

"I will have it for you in less than 45 minutes Great One."

I smile and turn to the others. Diana goes to the bags and grabs a small square object I know to be her laptop. Their models are much more advanced than anything Humans have, but it can only be used by someone who knows Kroh.

I turn to my two Human friends to find them looking at me and actually look uncomfortable. They really believe the exchange between Diana and I is a problem, when in fact it might have given me a few other ideas about my situation. I look at Brad and nod toward Diana now sitting at the table with her fingers flashing over the complex keyboard.

"I would like her to be part of my personal guard. It will be good to have one of the old races to talk to. Would that be alright with you?"

"Ah, yes, I guess. You are the boss after all. But I thought the exchange between you two was not going too well there."

"Actually Brad, in the days of the Empire, the Conranians and the Kroh were two close races, often working closely together to better the planets and the Empire. Since the Conranians were the oldest and the leaders, they were called Great Ones, while the Kroh were pretty much the brains behind most of the advancements, they were called Wise Ones. Also, their steady demeanor and even tempers made them better suited to evaluate situations without emotions affecting the outcome. That is part of the reason I would love to count her as my personal guard. Not only could her skills with technology come in handy, but her opinion on certain situations could make sure I don't act foolishly. How are her fighting skills? I ask because it is rare to see any Kroh as a soldier."

"She's one of the best on the field, for the reasons you mentioned, but she does have a temper and I pray for the soul of anyone she gets mad with, as it will leave them soon after. No one in the force wanted her on their team because of her race, but after talking to her for a few hours I saw something others did not. Passion. She has a passion to learn every single aspect of life, including fighting. Now every member of the team would give their life for hers, and she for them."

"Good. I hope one day to deserve that passion in her and the rest of your team. Now the real reason I wanted to see you is to talk about salaries. I am not familiar with what salaries should be for the personal guard of someone like me. Any ideas?"

"I'm not comfortable giving you numbers I think we should be paid, kind of feels like I would be taking advantage of your ignorance."

"overcautious, then how much does a normal guard, say at a bank, would make? Do you know?"

"I've known a couple that were not very satisfied with their conditions but they always stayed because the pay was good and they were paid fifty a year. But whatever you decide to pay us my team will be grateful. Working for a person such as what Geraldine tells me you are will be gratifying, at least much more than working for your late husband."

"Alright, so let's crunch up some numbers. A bank guard's only job is to protect the money and not really the employees. Your team will not only be protecting me but also my money, ships and all the other employees that will work for me. Of course, your team will grow much larger soon, but let's take this a step at a time. So, a bank guard makes between forty and fifty for protecting money, so your team for now should make at least seventy-five since you have much more to protect. As the team grows the other soldiers will probably start at a slightly lower salary while yours will grow. So, let's start the five men and women guarding us now at seventy-five, Diana as my personal guard and aide, will be at eighty, and you as their leader will start at one hundred. Does that sound fair to you?"

Before he can answer I can hear some excited talk at the door so I'm guessing they heard and like the proposal, while Diana barely slows down but the sudden hesitation means she has also heard. I hope it's enough for her to accept the dual job. Brad finally closes his mouth and answers.

"Well, my moral code has to mention that it is high, but if those are the salaries you are willing to pay, I'm sure my team and myself will accept."

"Hell yeah we'll accept boss!" says one of the guys by the door.

The man actually blushes at his outbreak as I look his way. It's funny seeing a man much bigger than Brad blushing at a small woman such as myself, but it makes me smile because he's not afraid to speak his mind but also knows he's out of line as a soldier.

"What about you Diana. Will this dual posting be acceptable for you?" I ask.

She only gives a slight nod and I can also see a small smile cross her lips before it disappears just as quickly. Good, now I have the start of my new team of close supporters and maybe even friends. Some would think it folly to spend over three quarter of a million credits on just eight people, but if you want to make sure the closest people to you cannot be bribed or corrupted, you need to take care of them as if they were family. My husband never understood that, now he's dead. I will not make that mistake. From the memories of the Conranian people I now have in my head, most were close nit and would give their lives for each other. I plan on continuing that system all the while not making the same mistakes the old generations did before they were destroyed.

Geraldine finished the contracts and one at a time they all come and sign as well as scan their fingerprints to the contract. They also give information on their accounts so the money can be deposited. I then ask silently Geraldine to transfer a year's worth in each account as a thank you for their service today, without which I would not be standing here. Brad leaves right after signing his own contract so he can start searching for more candidates. I leave him to decide the terms of their employment as I cannot micro manage every aspect of this new business I inherited. He's the leader of the guards, let him deal with his men and women.

A little shy of forty minutes after giving my new personal aid slash guard Diana announces that she has all the data I had asked. She has a smile of satisfaction at the time she has achieved, as well she should, but I cannot tell her that as it would be a show of none confidence in her abilities, so I give the proper response for the great work she's done.

"Maybe next time I might have to give you a tighter time frame."

The large smile, although uncommon among her kind, speaks loud and clear. She is proud of her work and knows I am too. The problem I now face is going through the data she has for me. I will definitely need more aids.

22

3

Chapter 3

We start by going through the ships here on this planet. Thinking it would take only a few hours was optimistic as we are now in the third hour and barely have a quarter of the ships finished. The problem is that for each ship, we need to check its capabilities, cost, repair cost if any, and then go through all the personnel files. We mainly start with the officers and see if we need to dig further. A good Captain will rarely keep bad crew on board. But with twenty-six ships in system, the task is far greater than expected.

Fortunately, the new members of my personal guard are much more than just soldiers. Each has his or her specialty, and all contribute their input on the personnel, the ship conditions and what role best suits it. Of all the property I've inherited, the ships are the only thing I actually care about. There is something about owning a company that my tyrant husband had that gives me the creeps, so I ask Geraldine to come up with a solution for selling all of the assets I now own except the ships. She has been at her computer for the whole time, never coming up except to eat the delicious lunch Aaron has made for us.

Aaron Lombardy is of Italian descent and has the natural culinary talents his ancestors on Earth had. He's the one that had shouted that they accepted the contracts. He had inherited other traits of his ancestors, one of which was being loud. It was a wonder the other floors didn't hear him talk of anything from food to the cute girl he saw in the lobby to the state of the bathrooms in the same lobby. He could have bothered me with his loud voice, but he's so damn joyful all the time that all you do is smile.

Aaron's best friend in the group is Hector Fernandez, a smaller man of Hispanic descent. He is so quiet compared to his friend that you can easily think him a mute, but he puts his grain of salt into the conversation once in a while, usually to unravel whatever crap Aaron is trying to spring on the rest. He's about my height, but with broad shoulders and very strong arms. His biceps are about the size of my waist. He seems shy compared to his friends but Diana has assured me when it comes to combat, he turns into a fearless warrior.

The last man on the team is Rjoart. He's Xirtan, a warrior race that fights for peace. Most races of similar definition will only say peace so they can rule the others, but the Xirtan do not wish to lead, only keep the peace. Although almost childlike compared to his companions at only five feet seven and barely a hundred and fifteen pounds, I'm assured that none of them would fight him in unarmed combat unless they had help from at least two more people. From what I already know and from what the knowledge given to me by the power remembers, if the Xirtan wanted to take over the old Empire or the present Alliance, they could have done so easily.

So why had they not come to the rescue of the Conranian

Empire back then? Because the Vuldalian had poisoned their homework before invading and had sent nerve agents on the planet to either kill or cripple the population, preventing them from taking part in the war. Rjoart is barely into adulthood for his race at seventy-eight years old. The eldest known Xirtan to still be alive is three hundred and eighty-five and still going strong.

The two remaining members of the team are women, or one of them is, the other might be debatable. Julie Fortin is good looking, with beautiful eyes and smile. Her Canadian descent gives her the innocent happy and polite personality typical of the old Earth inhabitant of that Country, but it also gives her the fire inside that spills out whenever someone threatens her family, or extended family. Everyone remembers the Canadians for being nice and polite people, but most seem to forget that back before they left the home world for space, they created a game played on ice. In this game the inner rage all Canadians have would come out whenever someone wronged a player on their side and fights would break out, some of which were extremely violent. From what I learn, Julie is a very big fan of Hockey, the game her Country created. I pity the men who treat her badly.

And finally, we come to Weil, the only member of the team that would not pass for a Human at a quick glance. Weil is a Brandari, a race that has no gender, no hair or body hair, seven slender fingers, four arms and a body mass that doubles what a normal humanoid would weigh at comparable size. Brandari are great healers, their four arms and extra fingers giving them an edge over conventional human-like beings. Their eyes are capable of something similar to infra-red vision, giving them the ability to see infections in a patient before the computers tell them so.

Another not so known fact about the Brandari is their ability to get information out of people. Their medical background lets them know exactly where to apply pressure for pain, pleasure, or any other sensation they wish to induce in their target. They make the best doctors but also the best interrogators. To have one in your unit, let alone your personal guard is a luxury not many can brag about.

I've asked Hector to locate the best suitable ship for my personal use in the ones that are in system. After looking at all the data, he comes to me with his findings.

"My best choice would be this one, *The Widow*. I didn't choose it for the name, although it fits, but for many other reasons. First it looks like a regular transport ship, not too luxurious and has an excellent complement of weapons and armor. Probably was a raider ship before your husband got his hands on it. We can put in a week of work on it and make it comfy and look more like the main ship of someone of your stature."

From the looks of shock on the other's faces, I'm guessing he's never talked so much in their presence. Brad's words as he comes back in confirm my thoughts.

"Hector, it's a wonder you're not gasping for air after all that speech."

Hector blushes beet red at all the attention he's getting, so I lean in a bit and give him a small kiss on the cheek.

"Excellent choice Hector, I love it. Get a team of mechanics and anyone else you need and have it done, but not too fancy."

"Actually Sherry-Ann that will have to wait." Brad says.

"Trouble already?"

"Yes, in the form of the President. I got in the elevator before he could see me but right now it should be stopping in the lobby and bringing him up with his goons. Do you want this messy or silent boss?"

"Actually, none of those options should be necessary. Geraldine, do you have the list I asked you to look into earlier?"

She hands me a tablet with all of the companies I now own in system. Most are on the surface but a few mines across the system are also on the list. An inkling of a plan is forming inside my head, but it's not complete yet. Time to take step one and make things happen.

"Rjoart, would you please stand guard at the door? Don't stop them coming in, just make sure no more than two guards come in with the President."

The Xirtan nods and walks slowly toward the door. I look at the rest of the team getting ready for battle.

"Guys, please sit in the living room and continue your research in our new ships and crew. With Rjoart as a guard nothing will happen to me, and I would like to keep this meeting peaceful. I may need some allies one day, and a system President might make a good first option."

None of them moves until I look Brad in the eyes and he nods to his team. Good, they don't obey blindly, they make sure my safety is assured before doing anything foolish. Brad knows that I'm right, or at least he understands what I'm trying to do.

Rjoart silently coughs so I know the President is coming and I see his fingers moving behind him to indicate to Brad and myself that six guards are with my guest. He doesn't move at all as the President walks besides him without a glance. He probably dismisses him as a kid or nothing of worry. The first two guards also walk by without problem but when the next one moves to follow, he's blocked by a sword so shinny I could almost see myself in it even at this distance. The guard moves his arm to swat it away but in the blink of an eye finds himself on his ass with a sword a hair from his jugular. The other three outside the apartment try to go for their weapons but Rjoart turns so fast as he whips out a second sword that none see the move before their now useless weapons fall to the ground in two pieces. The first sword has never left the third guard's throat since it first connected, and now the President and his guards are weary.

"Don't worry Mr. President he's harmless, unless you happen to threaten me or disobey one of my wishes."

"And just what wish did we disobey?"

"The one about you being able to enter with only two guards. That third one wanted to join the party but he's not invited, and neither are the other ones. If your guards will retreat toward the elevator my man will remove his sword from your guard's throat and you will have saved four lives today, at the least."

He nods to his guards and all four retreat toward the elevators. I nod at Rjoart and he places himself in the middle of the doorway looking at them. None of these four will ever make the mistake of underestimating a smaller man ever again, I think.

"Please join me in the living room President Fuentez. I find it more comfortable for a business meeting than sitting in the hall."

I walk toward the living room, not even caring about him or his guards. I somehow know that as much as Rjoart is watching the men outside, the six other members of my guard are scrutinizing what the three men behind me are doing. One wrong move by any of them and the life would be out of them before they fell to the floor. As expected, I enter the living room and all six are standing around the seating area, arms at the ready all the while looking relaxed. The three men following me give a quick glance at each other before going for seats. Brad and Weil block the way of the two guards while

Alvaro Fuentez sits opposite me in the comfortable couches.

"You seem to have powerful friend Miss McDonald."

"Lebronski."

"Pardon me?" Alvaro asks.

"My name is Sherry-Ann Lebronski. McDonald was my late husband's name, one I no longer wish to be associated with. Now, what do I owe the honor of your visit to my suite President Fuentez?"

"Well, I was…" he stammers as he looks at all the guards around him.

"Since you seem at a loss for words, let me open the conversation with a proposal I was thinking of going to see you with. I now own fourteen companies on the surface of Alexandria as well as three mines and two mining facilities in space. The net worth of all these together is seven hundred sixty-two billion credits, not counting the five mining ships that move the ore from the mines to the facilities. So, make it seven hundred seventy billion in total. I now find myself wanting a new direction in my life and would like to offer you the chance to enrich your life a bit and make a real difference in the system."

The President looks at me as if I have two heads and six arms. No sane person would sell the property I am offering him. All are very profitable and grow in value every year. I'm not sure of my end game but I know it does not include these properties. If I can make a good amount of money and make a friend in the process, this could be worth even more than the money it gives me.

"That's quite an offer you're making Miss Lebronski. And how much would you be asking for these properties and ships?"

The fish is hooked, now to pull him in slowly so as not to lose him. He probably came here intent on avenging a person he believes was a friend and might now leave a very rich man and have a real friend instead of someone using him and pretending to be a friend.

"First, I know you don't have nearly enough credits to pay any price I ask of you, so stop thinking you'll get this deal for pennies on the dollar as they used to say back on old Earth."

"How do you know how much wealth I have hidden all over the place?"

At my nod Diana walks forward and pulls out her tablet.

"You have barely forty million credits in your several accounts, and if you sold all your stocks and other equities your wealth would only climb to fifty-three million credits. A nice amount given that you only work as President, but not even enough to give a deposit I believe." Diana says.

His mouth almost to the floor he almost sounds like a child wining about a broken toy.

"Your husband told me he had a sizable percentage put away for me in his files."

"He never mentioned anything of the likes to me sir, and I managed every credit that went through his properties." Geraldine mentions.

"Then what kind of a deal do you plan to offer me?"

"I plan to give these companies and ships to you."

Again, his mouth is further to the floor, but it's now joined by all present except me. Time to pull the fish out of the water for good.

"The properties and ships in this system make an average profit of fifty-two billion per year. Were you to accept the deal, you will take no more than one percent of the profits for your salary. That will grow your fortune to ten times what you have now per year. You will pay me a percentage of the profits for the companies. The rest will be divided between profit charring with the employees, repairs and replacement of faulty equipment, a security fund in case of a bad year, and a new research and development department that will focus on developing technology that I will suggest to you."

Now the politician comes out as I talk his language, money.

"overcautious, so one percent for me, that sounds more than reasonable. How much would you take?"

"Twenty percent."

His eyes pop out of his head, but he collects himself.

"Is the amount negotiable?"

"Nothing I'm offering is negotiable. You either take it the way I present it or you don't take it at all."

"Fine, how would the profit be divided? I'd like to know what I'm getting into before agreeing to this."

Good, he didn't go right away for the five hundred and twenty million credits a year. That means he has a sense for business as no deal is perfect.

"First your one percent, my twenty percent, profit charring at ten percent, equipment maintenance will cost you about five percent per year, twenty-five percent for the security fund, which leaves thirty-nine percent for R&D. It might seem a lot for you on simple research, but I promise you that the projects

I will have you research will probably double the profit in the next ten years."

"That sounds all good in a conversation, but do you have data that I can look at and also have my own accountant look at?"

"Call him or her now so they can join us."

"What if he's busy?"

"Mr. President, this could give you a minimum of five hundred million credits a year, I'm sure you can make it worth his while."

He takes out his comm and dials. He walks away a bit to have a private conversation, but unknown to him, and me before today, Alan had listening devices all over the apartment and thanks to Diana I now have access to them via a small ear piece.

"Rick, drop everything you're doing and get to Alan's penthouse. Grab your computer on the way up."

"I'm with my mistress Alvaro, I can't just leave like that?"

"For the love of whatever God you pray to, if it's mistresses you want, you'll be able to afford tons of them."

"Look man, this is Charlene, you know the one I talked to you about last week. I can't…"

"If you're not here in thirty minutes I personally call your wife and give her the numbers of all your mistresses." And he hangs up.

He walks back to us and sits back down. Before he can say anything, I let him know my priorities about respect.

"I will let you bring this filth in my Penthouse this once so he can authenticate the numbers, but if you agree to this deal, you'll have to find someone more reputable. A man that has several mistresses and a wife is not one I want in my organization or of ones I deal with. You seem like an honest politician if that even exists, so know that men like Alan was are not welcome, or women for that matter. Anyone that doesn't oblige to the code of conduct of respectful dealings with others will have a meeting with one of my friends here."

Aaron sits, no drops, next to Alvaro and grins at him.

"That also goes for the people that do not denounce them. I love pounding on idiots before breakfast."

Julie walks slowly and sensually toward Alvaro.

"And Mr. President, we'll find out if anyone's cheating the rules. We have ways of finding them." She finishes while trailing a finger on his chin and grinning at him.

Alvaro looks aroused and scared shitless at the same time.

Finally, the accountant walks in, looking all around and wondering what all this is about, then sees Alvaro and walks to him.

"What the fuck's going on here? I thought Alan got killed in that explosion."

"Indeed, he did." I say getting up from the couch and walking toward him. His eyes trail all over my body and I can sense every member of my guard tensing, until I shake one finger behind my back. I need this deal to go through, and without this poor excuse for a man, it might go down the drain.

Alvaro explains quickly what he needs this guy to look through and they sit down to do that. It takes four hours for the accountant to give a quick look at all the numbers and find them in favor of Alvaro accepting the deal. The President shushes him out before he can do any damage with his sleazy hands, but it's too late, as Julie walks slowly in front of the man. They intend on showing the President what could happen if he breaks the rules of respect I intend to apply.

33

The accountant walks up to her and before even talking to her grabs her ass. In the blink of an eye the man loses that very hand to a sharp blade held by Julie herself. I can feel the pressure building inside me again as I see this pervert just pushing himself onto my new friend. The man screams and goes for a blaster, but he never gets the chance to even clear it from his jacket as I extend a hand and the electrical power that had come earlier in the day now races toward the accountant and before anyone can blink it's over, the man gone and a pile of ash lies at the place he stood. Rage in my eyes, I turn toward the President with a smile.

"Looks like you won't have a choice to find yourself another accountant even if you don't accept my deal."

"What are you, a witch?" he says, horror in his voice.

"No, worse. I'm Conranian."

His eyes grow larger than I thought possible and then he turns to where Geraldine is standing and asks for the tablet with the contract. Phase one is now started.

4

Chapter 4

The next week goes by so fast that I can barely remember sleeping. Hector has assembled a large group of mechanics, engineers and laborers to retrofit the main ship I now call the Red Widow, and it's now standing proud in the warehouse with its brand-new red paint job, same color as my hair.

Most of my week has been interviewing the officers of all twenty ships left in my group that are in system. With five mining ships now in the ownership of Alvaro, and my beauty on the tarmac in front of me, the twenty ships left count a total of over six hundred crew, but only ninety-five officers. When most of the officers that did not make the cut are dealt with, nicely for the most part, I asked the guard to walk through the ships and inspect them for bad apples.

Today is the day that I finally see the inside of my new ship and meet the crew. Hector insisted that I remain out of the bay so that I could be surprised when I saw my baby. Well, the outside is spectacular, and I can't wait to see what the inside looks like. Finally, Hector walks out of the airlock and begs me to follow him to the back where a large ramp makes its way down to the floor of the bay. Hector and Brad had interviewed all the crew for my main ship personally to make sure all are top notch.

I follow Hector to the back and I can hear heavy footfalls and see the ramp shaking from something heavy hitting it repeatedly. I'm surprised to see the enormous creature walking down the ramp in what can pass for a uniform for his race. The Fernonian is big even for his race, and these rock creatures are large. This one looks to be just shy of eight feet and has an impressive assortment of weapons across his body. Since Hector does not seem bothered by the large man, I should not either, but history between the Fernonians and Conranians has not been the most pleasant. It's a wonder he even agreed to work for me.

The mountain stops at the base of the ramp as we reach it and bows when he seems me.

"Sherry-Ann, this is Hank Ionicci, your head of security aboard the Red Widow."

"It is a pleasure to serve under you Madam." Hank says in a voice like two mountains grinding against each other.

"A pleasure to have you Hank. Please call me Sherry-Ann, or even just Sherry. I hate formalities. And please do not bow to me. I'm not the leader of the Alliance or anyone special."

Hank gets back up to his full height and it hurts my neck just to look into his eyes.

"The ship is ready sir and secure. I've had my team search it four times since yesterday to make sure no one interfered with any systems."

"Excellent Hank, thank you. Sherry-Ann, shall we?" he asks waving his hand toward the interior.

I reply by walking up the ramp. Hector walks up next to me

while my walking mountain walks a few feet behind us and his eyes search every corner of the ship. I don't think anyone would dare hurt me with him back there, but it makes me feel safer knowing that a Fernonian heads my safety. Although our people's history has been in conflict most of their existence, once a Fernonian gives his protection and loyalty to someone, he will die before any harm comes to his charge.

The first thing I notice is the ship smells new, with fresh paint on the walls, new flooring or at least old one polished to perfection, and the lifts in the cargo area are new. Several members of my new crew are in the cargo bay and most stop what they are doing for a second to salute and then go back to work. All have military precision to their movements, and it seems someone had uniforms made as all have the same clothing except for small differences. Those are probably for ranks, postings and the like.

I smile as I can easily see myself roaming the stars with this ship, but that will be for another time. We walk the large ship for another fifteen minutes as Hector explains this system or that, all the while I mainly notice that every corridor is high enough for my shadow to walk perfectly straight. His eyes have not stopped moving even in the middle of the ship and I'm starting to think that they never stop.

"Would you like to see the bridge, Sherry?" Hector asks.

"Oh yes I would."

Hector takes the lead and directs us toward a lift. As we wait for it to arrive, I turn toward Hank.

"Hank, may I ask a question of you."

"You may Madam."

"Sherry Hank, please."

"Yes Madam."

"What made you take this posting?"

"If you're referring to the bad blood between our two races in the past, I've never been one to keep a grudge that doesn't affect me personally. Our ancestors were idiots it seems as two races as strong as ours should have joined together instead of fighting each other. The universe would be better with less violence."

The lift arrives and we walk in. As soon as Hank walks in I can almost hear the whining of the motors as it takes us to the bridge level. As we arrive at the good level the door opens but Hank holds out his hand out before I can move. I'm about to ask him what he's doing when a runaway cart flies by with a person on board. That person seems unconscious and will hurt someone if not controlled. I push past Hank, a feat in itself, and extend my hand toward the cart. It slows down quickly and then stops completely just before slamming into a group of officers. A young woman runs by almost out of breath. She has a different uniform as others.

"Officer Blanche, what's going on?" Hank rumbles.

"Sir, not sure yet. The cart slammed into Al and knocked him out. I've been chasing it seems for an hour but probably is only a minute."

"You're out of shape it seems. I want you to hit the exercise room every morning for an hour before your shift, am I clear?"

"Yes sir."

"I also want you to find out what caused this cart to almost crash into the Admiral."

For the first time Stephanie notices me and goes white. She salutes and then runs away from us.

"A little harsh there Hank?" I say.

"Yes Admiral, but Stephanie is a gifted security agent. I've seen her outrun many opponents, so for her to be out of breath like this means she needs a little extra in the gym. She's gained a bit of muscle after the military, so she still has to get used to carrying the extra weight around. Nothing like hitting the gym to help that."

"There's something I've always wondered about your race. Do you guys need to hit the gym to have your strength? I mean, does it give you more rocks or is there some kind of muscle tissue under that hard surface."

"Yes, we do, as your second hypothesis is the correct one. And by fighting our outside shell becomes thicker and stronger."

"Do you mind me asking Hank?"

"Not at all Admiral. Most people do not ask simply because they are afraid of our size, but we are really a gentle race."

"What is your rank among my crew?"

"Commander Admiral."

"Very well Commander, may I ask another question of you? I do not want to bother you with all my questions, but it's the first time I meet a Fernonian and I want to make sure I do not offend you in any way."

"You can ask me anything Admiral Lebronski, my heart and soul are an open book."

"Are there a lot of your race that travel the systems in other than the Royal Guard?"

"Not many, Admiral. It is frowned upon by my people to mix with the other races, but more and more are seeing as I do, that we can only become stronger when we exchange thoughts and knowledge."

"I believe I will ask you to join me for dinner tonight so we may continue this conversation. I find your outlook on life very satisfying and would love to share ideas with you. Will you join me, but not as Commander Ionicci, but as Hank?"

"It will be my pleasure Admiral."

"And tonight, I want you to call me Sherry, not Admiral."

"Yes Admiral."

"Excellent Commander. Now Hector, this trip to the bridge is taking us much longer than I expected."

"Actually Sherry-Ann, we've been going in circles for the last few minutes because we got here almost right out of the lift but your conversation with Hank was also very interesting for me so I wanted to listen to it."

"Then maybe you can join us as well for dinner, if the Commander does not object."

"Not at all, I've grown fond of Commander Fernandez in the last week."

"Excellent, the more the merrier. Now onto the bridge."

The door opens as I walk close to it and I enter what can only be called controlled chaos. It seems the new equipment Hector had installed is so new that most of the crew have to re-learn their jobs. Each shift officer is at their post making sure they are up to date on everything before we ship off. The only calm person on the bridge is the captain. Not very tall, and she looks young for the rank, but although her demeanor is calm, her eyes scan everything and nothing goes unnoticed. I see a pad next to her that she scribbles on once in a while, and no one bothers her for anything.

I approach her chair and as soon as I'm close, I go to open my mouth but her left hand strikes up and she holds it in my face to stop whatever I'm about to say. A little annoyed I'm about to let her know my thoughts but then I hear it, the faint clatter on the right, close to the ceiling of the bridge. I can feel the power inside me again and I seem to have more control over it now so I send a trickle of power to the loose part and make sure the screw is tight in seconds. I see the captain's eyebrow rise, and then she does the same and faces me.

Hank goes for introductions but she simply looks at him and he backs off. I like her already.

"Admiral." She says, no bow, nod or any other sign of respect.

"Captain." I answer in the same way.

Then I nod to her slightly and she extends her hand.

"Elena Ross Madam. Thank you for that, it was driving me crazy and disturbing my concentration."

"Sherry-Ann Lebronski, and it's my pleasure. I can see how something as simple as a loose screw can completely take you off your game. You have to wonder if it will fall at the wrong moment and screw everything. Small things are far worse than large problems."

"A woman after my own heart. I like you already Admiral. Now the rules of the ship when it comes to you. Anywhere but the bridge you outrank everyone but me. You may go anywhere you choose and at whatever time. On the bridge, all Officers outrank you while at their station. You need something you ask, you do not order. The ship is mine so as long as you're on board, I order you and not the other way around. Off ship you are my superior and I will give you all the respect you deserve."

"I would not have it any other way."

"Good, then we'll get along splendidly. Now I need to prepare for departure. Hector had a seat installed on my left for you so you can see and hear everything, but away from the main screen in case of communications. Is that acceptable?"

"It is. Would I be able to observe the liftoff and stay for a while after?"

"You can come and go as you please, as long as you do not disturb any of the officers when they are working."

Elena turns around and goes back to her chair, a smile on her lips. I really like her. She's strong and confident, a testament to women everywhere. I nod to my two escorts and Hector leaves the bridge while Hank retreats to the bridge door and stands at attention. I have a feeling that as long as we're in the bay, or at a station somewhere, Hank will be my shadow to make sure nothing happens to me.

The rest of the day goes by really fast as I immerse myself in the bridge activity and try to listen more than anything. I've never been on the bridge of any ship, but my memories give me enough information about each station that I can grasp most of the information being said back and forth. By mid-afternoon Elena announces that we are ready to depart the bay as well as the rest of the fleet. That single word triggers more memories that I will have to think deeper on later tonight, but for now the view out the main screen is all I need to satisfy my joy of life I found in the last week.

The ship lifts off with more smoothness I would think a ship of this size would be capable. The pilot directs it toward the large bay's exit and soon we find ourselves out in the open air and surrounded by twenty other ships, my ships.

Four smaller ships take point and spread out to cover any enemy that would think to attack them. On each side of the Red Widow, I can see on a small monitor attached to my chair that six larger ships mix their positions to cover us on all vectors. The last four ships take the rear and have a similar size as the ones in the front. I will need to study each ship's capabilities if I can understand how to utilize them best. Soon we hit the outer atmosphere and I can barely feel any vibrations but the memories tell me it will change once we re-enter an atmosphere.

Then the beauty of space becomes visible and I can barely pull my eyes from the main screen. Out of the corner of my eye I can see Elena looking at me so I turn her way.

"First time in space Admiral?"

"It is, although I have memories I now believe belong to my ancestors of them being into space quite often, but none of them could have prepared me for its beauty."

"Now you know why we do it. The call to space sets in very early in your career and after a few years being dirt side feels foreign and space like home. Did I hear correctly that you're hosting a dinner tonight? Mind if I join you guys?"

"I would love that. How did you hear about it?"

"Nothing stays secret aboard a ship Admiral. Oh, and thanks by the way for saving Al. My baby brother is a wiz when it comes to ships and other technology, but clueless around people. He probably got knocked over because someone was talking to him, most probably a girl."

"My pleasure. Well, there was a security officer there, Stephanie."

"Ah, that explains it. She's cute as hell and Al probably has the hots for her."

"You do not frown on crew members flirting with each other?"

"Nope. As long as they do their duty first and their feelings do not interfere with the ship's function, I don't see why I should stop what's gonna happen anyway. This way it's all done out in the open where I can control things instead of in hiding."

"And any man you have an eye on Captain?"

She lowers her voice and bends a bit to her left so as not to be heard.

"That security Commander back there, your shadow, I'd do some nasty things to him."

This woman was weird. First in public she's strict, business like, but as soon as she's in her element and more comfortable, she turns into a talking machine, one that apparently loves rough sex.

"You do know Captain that Fernonians have incredible hearing ability, so knowing him I'm pretty sure he now knows you want to have some fun."

She looks scared behind them and then back at the main screen, a little red on her cheeks. I look back at Hank and he gives me a small smile. He heard.

The fleet heads for one of the jump points when Elena turns again toward me, but the business-like Captain is speaking now.

"Destination Admiral?"

"Glengarry system."

Elena looks at me funny but then repeats it to her navigator, even though he heard clearly what I had said. Her ship indeed. Jump points are neutral points in the system where the pull of the sun, planets and any other body will not affect the ship and rip it apart when it goes to jump space. I sit back and relax before I live through my first jump space experience. Ten minutes before arriving at the jump point, I get the feeling something's not right. It's not exactly a premonition as I can't tell what will happen, but something will for sure. I reach for Elena's arm.

"Something's not right Captain."

"In what way? I know you Conranians have special powers, but I need more than not right."

"Several large ships entering the system at the jump point Captain!" the sensor officer says.

"Now we know what your something is." She tells me. "Battle stations everyone, all ships to go to full alert. I want all weapons hot and ready yesterday. Shields up and I want the Admiral in the battle room Commander even if you have to carry her there."

"I will not…" I start to say but Hank grabs me around the waist and the only way to break his grip would be to use my power on him but I do not plan to do so. The battle room it turns out is not even on the same section as the bridge. It has a secondary bridge, where in the event that the bridge is open to space and all are dead, the people in here can continue the fight and escape. We enter the room to find the second bridge shift already at their stations and the third one at the back of the room in case they're needed. The main chair is for me and I sit in it. Hank motions for the headset on the side of the chair and I place it on my head.

"Glad you could join us Admiral." Says Captain Ross in her ear. "I wanted you out of the bridge because if we fall you need to be able to save the rest of the fleet. And of course, this way you can give me any input you have on what you can see on the numerous screens."

"So, you still look like you're giving the orders, keep the respect of the crew and have an extra pair of eyes, one that is not preoccupied with flying the ship."

"You learn fast Admiral. Now tell me what you see while I prepare to face what comes out of the jump point."

I take a few seconds to view all the screens available, my new

45

memories making it capable for me to comprehend data a lot quicker.

"Our formation is fairly strong, but I would place *Johnson's Goddess* and the *Star Fortress* closer to the front to support the faster and more agile ships. This way while they harass the enemy the gunships can dish out some serious punishment."

"Nice observation Admiral. You've got a good brain for tactics. Let's implement the Admiral's suggestion team and get ready for what comes out. Hopefully this will all be a false alarm."

"Captain, I thought the point of placing me in here was for you to keep credit for anything I might say."

"In the future it might be" she explains in a soft voice, "but the crew don't know you at all and I need them to understand that you're not just a pretty face with tons of money. This way they follow a leader, not a rich bitch."

I look at the monitors and screens and soon see the two ships I mentioned move forward just behind the small ships up front. The ships finally emerge from jump space and a fleet of eleven large ships appear in front of us and right away raise their shields. Right after all ships are being hailed.

"This is Captain Ross from The Red Widow Group, how may I be of service today?" I sense a barely restrained smile in her voice. I have a feeling she likes kicking ass.

"This is Rick Anderson and you're stealing my friend's ships. Be ready to be boarded."

"I'm sorry mister Anderson but we're not stealing anything. Since mister McDonald's death, all his property and belonging are now property of Admiral Sherry-Ann Lebronski, his widow."

"That bitch doesn't own anything. Alan would never leave

anything to one of his prostitutes."

Before Elena can reply both gunships fire everything they have at the two farthest ships that moments later, despite shields and good armor, explode in a spectacular fashion. Elena gets back on the comm.

"I would not use that kind of language around us mister Anderson. We are quite fond of our new employer and dislike people saying bad things about her. Now as you can see, we have plenty of firepower to overtake your little fleet and would love to show you more, but we have places to be. Anything else to add?"

"Prepare to die." He snarls before disconnecting.

His ships fire everything they have at our ships but all of them have already started moving in all directions. It seems all Captains have combat experience as none panic or need to be told what to do. The only weird formation is the four ships at our back that speed forward and then suddenly jump out of the system. I can hear Elena swear but she keeps it to herself. I look quickly at the captains for these ships and they are all ex-criminals, smugglers from the same group. I tear my eyes from that information and concentrate on the here and now, as I will have plenty of time to find these four ships later.

The battle goes well but our ships have suffered some damage, except for ours. What is Elena doing.

"Elena, why are we not in the fight."

"I'm protecting you Admiral, that's my job." She replies, although she doesn't seem to like it.

"Well, if you don't find a way to protect me in the middle of this fight all the while kicking some asshole ass, I might be forced to find another Captain."

"I was hoping you were gonna say that."

47

All of a sudden, the ship lurches to the right and thrusters go to full power. I can now hear missiles being fired as well as the enormous ship size Gauss rifles fire and the shields on the target ship go down momentarily. At that time the gunner has all the lasers on the ship fire at that point and the ship blows out a few decks of oxygen and a few gun ports. I can also feel several projectiles hitting the *Red Widow* but that is inevitable when in a fight like this.

All of a sudden four ships arrive at the jump point on full power and weapons hot and firing. It seems the four smugglers have a few tricks up their sleeves that we'll have to talk about once we get out of this. The four ships are firing on two of the larger ships from the back, hitting their engines and then moving on to the next as soon as the ships are disabled.

The battle lasts a few more seconds as most of Anderson's ships are either destroyed or incapacitated. Elena then tries to hail Anderson. A static filled screen comes on with him in the picture, his head bleeding but still alive.

"Hello again mister Anderson, not feeling so smug now, are you? I'm sure I speak for everyone when I tell you that the bitch might not mind having your surrender in person, on your knees, and bowing down to her. Might not be a bad idea also to lick her feet and maybe a few other things the fleet will think up before you arrive here."

"I will never surrender to that…" his words are stopped by a loud sound and a spatter of blood on the view screen. The lifeless body of Anderson is moved and then another person takes his place.

"My name is Kevin Waxman, first officer and now official leader of this group. We agree to surrender. What are the terms? I will do anything you wish, as long as you spare the crew of the ships."

"Admiral, you want to take this one?" Elena whispers.

"I would thank you." She then switches the frequency to be the one on Waxman's screen.

"Very good decision Captain Waxman. I promise that the crew of all ships will be treated fairly as long as they respect a few basic rules. No disrespect toward women, no infighting between crew, they follow my orders to the letter. If your crews are able to follow these rules, I might actually be nice enough to include you in my fleet of ships. For now, please care for your wounded and I will have teams of Marines board each ship. If your people so much as sneeze the wrong way toward my people they will be taken care of, if you get my meaning."

"I do miss?"

"Her name is Admiral Sherry-Ann Lebronski, and you better treat her with all the respect she is owed." Puts in Captain Ross with fire in her voice.

"Admiral, if anyone so much as think the wrong way, I will space them myself."

The connection cuts and I switch to fleet frequency.

"All Marines prepare to board the enemy ships. Be advised that they have surrendered and are to be treated with care for now. I will explain more in detail at a later date. Your contact is Captain Waxman. Captain Sillens, please take a team to their main ship and then on to the next until you have them all secured."

I switch back to my connection with Elena.

"Captain, might I suggest that we have an engineering team hook all the wrecks to some of our larger ships so we can move out of the way. Our trip to Glengarry will have to wait I'm afraid."

"Sounds like a plan Admiral. Might I suggest something as well?"

"Of course." I'm sure she'll suggest that I mind my own business.

"Invite the new Captain Waxman to your little dinner tonight."

"overcautious I'll bite, why would I want to do that?"

"This guy is ready to kill a billionaire in front of witnesses just so he can save his crew as well as that of the other ships. If I understand your thinking correctly, that's exactly the type of Officers you're looking for."

"Now I'm the one who likes your thinking. Would you mind doing the invite Captain?"

"I was thinking more along the lines of that hunk of a man behind you asking him. He's so charming after all."

5

Chapter 5

Although the *Red Widow* has an excellent cook I am told, I ask Aaron to prepare the meal for my special supper. I know Hank can protect me probably better than any of my security guard, I still like the fact of having the large Italian with me, if for nothing else than to intimidate the newly appointed Captain. I also ask Diana to come even if she doesn't talk much, she will be an extra protection if needed, although I doubt Captain Waxman will do anything to me after the stunt he pulled on the bridge of his ship.

As it turns out when I enter the private dining room appointed for this meal the whole gang decided to attend. When I walk in, I find Rjoart and Julie setting up the table, Hector and Weil placing flowers and other decorations for the dinner, and I also find a lot more places set than I thought would be attending. Looks like I won't have that quiet dinner with Hank to talk about his ideas. Oh well, I'll have plenty of time later in the trip, if Elena doesn't take him away from me that is.

The smells from the kitchen are wonderful and I make my

way there to see what the big man's got prepared for us tonight. As I open the hatch to the kitchen, I catch Aaron sampling some of his own food.

"And what are you doing there mister chef?"

"Just making sure the food's just right Sherry."

"With half a baguette in your hand and enough pasta sauce on it to feed four children?"

His only answer is a big smile as he continues the sampling. I look around at all the pots and pans, bowls and utensils all over the place and I pity the cleaning crew after the meal, but my taste buds can't take it anymore and I grab the baguette from his hands and dip a piece into the pasta sauce he was 'testing' and find it amazing. I just hope it's amazing enough to convince Kevin Waxman to join my cause. Out of the eleven ships that came out of the jump point, six are repairable. Those six large ships would be a great addition to the fleet of ships I will hopefully have by the end of my recon across my late husband's properties. Those ships are larger than any I have in this small fleet, and we were still able to defeat them. But used in conjunction with the smaller ships, they could be a great asset.

I walk back to the dining area to find the guard sitting and chatting with Elena. All have smiles on their faces as they talk and the conversation is light. I walk to my place, which it seems is at the head of the table, and smile to all.

"Elena, just before we eat and the rest of the guests arrive, how's the casualty report?"

"We have sixteen crew dead, close to fifty hurt but nothing serious. Considering the ferociousness of the short battle we just had, the count is good."

"Yes, but not good enough. I hate losing people, always had."

All look at me, as they all know I've never lead men and women in combat before.

"Sorry, the power I acquired not long ago came with not only knowledge but also with memories of people past. My guess is that they come from my ancestors somehow. It seems they did not like losing people then either."

"Well, that's good to know, that you come from a line of leaders that care for their crew. Now to finish my report before our guest of honor gets here. Damage to the ships in general is light, although the *Slasher* suffered a breach which accounts for most of the dead. I have crews trying to recover the bodies as we speak. Given that it's mainly an anti-fighter ship, it's a wonder that's it's still in working order against those large ships."

"Hector, please put a note to get a better shield system for it when we can, as well as all the other ships that need it. I want to reduce the amount of people we lose in the future."

Hector replies with a nod and soon the hatch opens and in comes Kevin Waxman followed closely by Hank. As soon as he walks into the room he goes to his knees and bows to me. I give Elena a dark look but all she does is laugh silently.

"Mr. Waxman, please get up. The bowing down and all was for your former boss, and it came from my Captain, not me."

"Come on Sherry, let him kiss your feet at least."

"I'm gonna have to watch out for you in the future miss Ross. Kevin, please get up and join us at the table. Aaron's been busy and I had the pleasure of sampling his food a few minutes ago and you're in for a treat."

The whole room erupts in cries of displeasure as they had been shushed away from the kitchen and threaten bodily harm if they touched the food. Kevin looks around at the group not believing his ears. I'm sure this never happened aboard the ship he was on. Those idiot billionaires think themselves so much better than everyone else, but they don't know the fun their missing.

"So, Kevin, any trouble with your crews? Sent anyone on a one-way trip?"

"No problem on my ship Admiral…" he starts.

"Kevin, this is a dining table, not a board meeting. My name here is Sherry, not Admiral."

"I'm not sure I can do that Admiral. I've been in Anderson's military for ten years now, and we could never think of his first name, let alone say it."

"Well, if Hank here is able to call me by my first name, surely you can. Hank?"

"Sorry Admiral." Hank says.

"Hank, you promised in the hall earlier that you would. Will I have to order you?"

The rest of the table is laughing hysterically, all but Kevin who at least has a smile on his face.

"No problems on my ship Sherry, but I can't say the same on the others. You should ask your gunships to make sure they target the *Revenge* and the *Fury*, both of which were securely under Anderson's control and mindset. All of us saw the damage your two ships did earlier, so if they keep a lock on the two ships, they should not try anything."

"And the other three?"

"They're on the fence I believe. The reason Anderson was on my ship was to keep me in line. He knew I didn't agree with his thinking."

"Do you think we should send more marines on the two ships mentioned?" ask Elena

"Might be a good idea."

"Rjoart, I saw on the crew manifests that a few of our ships have Xirtan on them. Do you know them?"

"I do." Is all he says. No need for more.

"Take two of the attack shuttles and assemble your team. I will leave those ships to you."

"I mean no offense Sherry, but I'm not sure a group of small man like him will…"

He never finishes as faster than the eye can see Rjoart gets up and has his sword under his chin. He had been on the other side of the large table.

"I stand corrected Sherry; they will do just fine." Kevin says, his voice scared.

Aaron comes out of the kitchen with some of his platters and the smell is enough to diffuse the tension. Rjoart takes his place back at the table and they eat while talking of various subjects for a few hours. Elena sent a message early in the meal to her XO to have the two gunships target the two ships and to leave the target active, all the while having officers at the ready at all times. Kevin eats in silence at first, shooting glances at Rjoart regularly, but soon relaxes and starts to talk more. By the end of the meal, he is laughing with the rest of the guests.

The dinner ends when barely half the food is consumed, so I ask Hank to bring it with him when he brings Kevin back to his ship.

"Thank you, Kevin, for your honesty in your answers, and your company at the table." I tell him while everyone exits the room and goes to their own duty.

"It was unexpected I have to say, but extremely enjoyable. I'm not sure I've ever had this much fun on a ship before."

"That's good. Part of the reason we invited you was to judge you and see how you might fit in our little group, but at the same time to spread the word to your people of what it's like to work for me. I may have more money than I will ever be able to spend, but I don't act like an ass like most billionaires do."

"You can count on the word spreading Sherry. I will gladly have my crew join you, and I will petition in your favor for the rest of the ships."

He leaves with Hank and I look around to find the whole room empty, so I sneak in the kitchen to get a glimpse of the mess Aaron might have left for the cleaning crew, only to find it spotless. Even the dishes we used are in the autowash and already halfway to being sanitized.

The next couple of days go by so fast I can barely believe the battle was three days ago instead of yesterday. Most of the external damage to the *Slasher* has been repaired and the ship is now jump worthy again. The rest of the damage will be completed either in transit or at a repair station at our next destination. The bodies of the sixteen dead have been recovered, as have many of the soldiers that attacked us and died in space. Kevin's ship is almost back to peek performance and his crew are as enthusiastic about joining my fleet as he was. Two more ships joined in a heartbeat, Kevin vouching for both. The two ships mentioned at dinner that could be trouble were, for a few minutes as Rjoart and his new team of master assassins made short work of the officers still loyal to Anderson. The bodies spaced as promised. The last ship joined, but Kevin warns that these officers might be serious trouble later.

Before we continue on our journey, I send loyal experienced

officers to the two offending ships to take control and evaluate the regular crew both in skill and in loyalty. I ask Rjoart to leave a few of his team on each ship to help with problems, and then ask him if he would mind going on another assignment right away, that of making sure the sixth ship will not become a problem. He agrees and slips in with a cargo of parts and that's the last I hear of him before we leave.

Before going I need answers to something that's been bothering me since the encounter. Most people knew of Alan's death by now, and I'm not surprised to see one of his old friends pop up in system like this, but with so many different jump points available, how did Anderson know which we would take. The easy answer would be Alvaro, but with the sweet deal we just signed, I'm not sure he would risk jeopardizing it for the likes of a guy like Anderson. Alvaro would not only lose the business he now had, but would probably be shot in the process.

I already had Diana check the log of every call made in the past week from the time we decided on our destination to the time of the attack, but she came up empty. Either the person was not part of my fleet or that person had a transmitter powerful enough to send a message to Anderson. But my thinking is more along the lines of someone ground side.

A tone announcing someone at the hatch sounds, and the computer tells me it's Diana. I give the order to enter and the hatch opens to a smiling Kroh. She really has a beautiful smile.

"I found him." She says before making it halfway to the desk.

She sits down uninvited and turns her computer toward me. Good thing I can now read Kroh. The language is extremely foreign to anyone used to English, but my brain translates the words in real time and I can read it as well as any English book.

"Who did you find Diana?" I reply, not making a note of the lack of regulation that she salutes when entering a superior's office.

"The person that sent the message. Alan, it seems had been on his way to see Anderson when his ship blew up, so when he got the news not long after, Anderson made his way here. A couple days later a tech loyal to Alan sent him a message telling him of work being done to Alan's ships, your ships by then. Anderson and he devised a plan for him to meet us at the jump point and blow us up. Bad idea after all. He sent the info on the jump point to Anderson when it was clear where we were going. Anderson, waiting just beyond the system was able to jump in quickly."

"Excellent work Diana. Please forward me this info, in English of course, and I'll call right away a friend to take care of the problematic tech."

Diana smiles and gets up, again forgetting to salute. She remembers just before getting to the hatch and turns with her best salute stance. I can see in her eyes that she knows she's made a grave mistake.

"Diana, I will never enforce the military policies when in private, especially when you have sensitive information like this to give. Don't worry about it."

She salutes again for good measure and then leaves. By this time I've received the file and dial my new good friend Alvaro Fuentez.

A nice female voice answers.

"Office of President Fuentez, how may I direct your call?"

"Good day, I need to talk to the President please." I ask nicely.

"The President is not taking any calls right now, may I take a message?"

"Please bother him and let him know it's Sherry-Ann Lebronski."

"Miss, it doesn't matter who…" she stops and then starts again in a whole new tone. "Oh, I'm sorry miss, I didn't recognize your voice, I'll get him right away for you."

"Before you do, how is he treating you at the office? Be honest please."

"Well, I do have to say that before you came along, I was basically a walking coffee machine, not very important to anyone, but since your meeting with him I've gotten a raise, and the way he talks to me has changed also. I feel important now."

"Did he ever mistreat you in any way?"

"Oh no, never President Fuentez. He's faithful to his wife. Your ex-husband on the other hand… Oh, I'm sorry I should not talk like that with you."

"No need to apologize, my ex was a pig of the worst kind."

"I'll get the President in a second for you."

I barely waited thirty seconds before Alvaro comes on the line.

"Sherry-Ann, everything alright? I didn't expect a call from you until you got out of jump space."

"Well, that's the thing Alvaro, we never got to jump space. It seems someone has been talking to Rick Anderson and he tried to take us out at the jump point."

"What! That slimy bastard won't know what hit him the next time he tries to make a deal with me."

"That's shouldn't be a problem anymore Alvaro, he was killed by one of his officers. I now own six new ships, although the crews might not all be thrilled about it."

"That's good news then. What can I do for you Sherry?"

"Two things. First, I'll send over a file containing the information on the technician that betrayed me to Anderson. I'll leave the details of what to do to him with you. Second, the scrap of five ships litters the space of the coordinates I just sent you along with the file. They will need a lot of work, but you might be able to put together one of two of them. Would give you some protection at least."

"How much do you want for the wrecks Sherry? Name your price."

"Nothing at all actually. I have plenty of ships and money, and you need protection. Call it a favor that one day I might ask for your help."

"You would have gotten my help anyway, but sure no problem. Safe travels."

The connection cuts and I relax in my chair. I check in with Elena and all the ships are ready for traveling. I hate having to give our destination to the ships that are not securely behind our cause, but there is nothing I can do about it. I did prevent communications of a sorts. Hector came to me not long after we assumed position a little off the jump point and suggested we block their comms. Of course, they would notice that, so I asked if there was any way to re-route them to our ship, to a specific computer so that we not only know they are communicating but we can respond.

Hector knew one of the techs on board with the skills to pull it off in a day so I gave him the go ahead to build one for each new ship. I had the tech, Augustine Henry, place the devices she created on the ships herself. She knew better than anyone where it would function best, and how to disguise them to look like they belong there.

Now ready, finally, for our first leg of the voyage, Elena

takes the ships to the jump point and engages the jump drive. I decide to look at it from my situation room instead of the bridge, so I'm able to see the beauty of jump space as well as all the data that flows through the screens. After a few hours of this unchanging view, I decide to explore the ship a little. Hank moves from his position by the hatch to follow, but I raise my hand.

"Commander, we are in jump space, no one but the crew is aboard, I think I can manage on my own and be safe. You do realize that I have power that exceeds anything you might have."

"I do realize that Admiral, but the Admiral cannot defend herself if someone surprises her with a blaster to the head from behind."

"Relax Commander, I'll be fine. Anyway, I will ask Lieutenant Gnalls to join me."

"If the Lieutenant joins you then I will feel safe enough to leave your side Admiral."

"Oh, and Commander, first shift is about to end."

"I realize that Admiral. Why do you mention it to me?"

"Because Captain Ross is on the first shift."

With that I walk out the hatch and walk toward Diana's quarters. She is the best companion when I feel like being alone, as she will not talk unless I do or I start a conversation, and if I have something to say that is not for all ears to hear, I can switch to Kroh. Of course, Hank will also not talk if I don't engage him in conversation, it's difficult to feel alone when you have an almost eight-foot mountain right behind you shaking the floor.

I soon find myself close to the quarters of my guard. I asked Hector to make sure all of them were close at hand in case I would need them for anything at a moment's notice. I'm so much into my own thoughts that I almost miss the warning signs screaming inside my brain. I whirl around in time to see the sword swinging for my head. I duct backwards and use the momentum to realize back to my feet and prepare an attack, but something grabs me all around and sends an electric shock through my body.

Normally I might have fainted, but years of being beaten by Alan have toughened me up quite a bit, but I let the assailant think I have fainted and drop to the floor.

"Not so tough after all bitch are you." The man says.

I don't recognize his voice so I don't believe I've met him. Then again, I haven't met most of the people on my fleet. I try not to move to give anything away but I wonder what his plan is. We are in jump space, aboard my ship, with almost all of the crew loyal to me. Someone will be looking for me soon and then they'll turn every corner out to find me. But then again, a lot of people loyal to Alan had been idiots. Alan loved those men as they were easy to manipulate and cheap to buy.

'Sherry, I'm close. What do you need me to do?' a voice says in my head. I then realize its Diana.

'I didn't know you could communicate telepathically but I'm glad. He surprised me in the corridor close to my room. He seems to be armed.'

'Do you want me to sound the alarm?'

'No, he might try to kill me right here if you do. He has an electrified net around me so I can barely move. He thinks I'm unconscious at the moment.'

'Perfect, let's give him another body to think of. When I make my move, get free and we can decide what to do with him afterward.'

'I'm ready.'

"Hey guys, I've got her but I'm gonna need help soon. Where are you?" the man says.

'Diana, wait! He's got some friends coming I believe. If we rush into this, we'll lose the chance to get them all.'

'Shit, already in the open. I'll improvise.'

"You finally got the bitch, good. What do you plan to do with her?" Diana says out loud.

The man gives a start and drops me, but I'm still stuck inside the net.

"Who the hell are you? Wait, you're that bitch's personal pet."

"Of course, how else could I get close enough to know all her weaknesses. The boss promised me I would take her place if I got rid of her, but she prevented me getting in his loving arms and now she has all his money. Trust me, I want her dead worse than you. What's your excuse?"

Diana was a good actor.

'You are acting I hope?'

'I would die before finding myself in the hands of a man like your ex, no offense boss.'

'None taken.'

"The boss hired me long ago to watch out for that prick Brad Sillens, but I wasn't fast enough to prevent him killing the boss."

"Is that what happened? Well now he needs to die as well. How many you got helping you, cause at this rate we'll have to take over the ship if we plan to survive long enough to enjoy seeing her suffer."

"He's got five people working with him bitch. Who are you?" some new voice calls.

"I'm her personal assistant. I was learning all I could to try and get that money away from her before I dispose of her. Got a problem with that?"

"I don't think so cutie. Me and my friends will dispose of her and then we'll have our way with you. You'll wish you were dead by the time we finish with that sweet ass of yours."

'Well that lasted as long as it could. The guard is on its way but won't make it in time. Can you get lose?'

'I believe so.'

'Do so now, it will create a diversion.'

The power builds inside me but I know it's too dangerous to use inside this narrow corridor, I might hit Diana. But then an image appears inside my head of a sword made of light and energy. Now you're talking. I let the power loose and the sword materializes in my hands cutting the net around me at the same time.

Diana takes this moment to jump in the middle of the five new men and swings a kick to one in the jaw, knocking him out cold. The man that attacked me takes his sword out and swings it at me but my own power sword blocks the blow and cuts into his blade to slice it in two and render it useless. I continue the move and switch angles a bit to slice into his throat. The man dies the instant the blade hits him, but no blood gushes out of his wound as the power burns the cut as it passes through flesh.

Diana has another man down but the other three have her defending herself and she will son run out of strength so I rush to her help and lose the blade and create energy around my fists. One of the men sees me and turns to intercept me but finds himself flying toward the end of the corridor as the energy in my fist slams into him. He's not out of it but has trouble getting up. I turn to another man as Diana slams a fist into the other's guts and continues her barrage of fists until he backs into the opposite wall. The man facing me tries to hit me across the face but my fist of energy grabs his and the man starts screaming as steam comes out of his ears, mouth and every other hole his body has. When the energy inside him becomes too much for the existing holes, his body makes more and the guy collapses in front of me, the smell of charred meat coming to my nose.

The man that had ended up at the end of the corridor tries to turn away but a large Italian grabs him by the hair and lifts him clear off the ground. He brings him closer to us and doesn't notice the screams the man is directing at him.

"Where do you want this one Admiral?"

"Find an empty corner of the ship, where no one else is, and take him to the farthest place from there. I want his interrogation to be public. I want everyone that thinks he can betray me and try to hurt one of my friends to hurt like hell and remember even in his next life not to fuck with me."

The anger in my voice even scares me, but it needs to be done. Aaron looks at me with a large grin on his face.

"Weil will do the interrogation."

The man's fear doubles as he understands that a Brandari will use their skills against him. Aaron on the other hand looks disappointed.

"Weil, please leave the man alive. I'd like Aaron to have a little fun with him as well. After all he did cook up one hell of a meal the other day."

His grin is back in place as he leads him by the hair and follows Weil.

As it turns out, the man is only a follower, but the man

Diana knocked out at the beginning is the leader so I ask Weil to get info out of him and leave the other guy as well as another still alive to the others. But as Weil starts her interrogation, I thought most people would leave, but a lot of off duty personnel start coming into the small room and ask to have their go at the traitors. I hesitate in answering but the guard take the decision for me and ask the people to line up. It's the craziest thing I've ever witnessed, people lining up to beat up traitors that tried to hurt me.

The show of hatred toward them in the eyes of the crew is equal to the love for me I see when they turn their eyes after hitting the men. I feel I should stop this somehow, but I'm not sure how to do so without hurting the feelings of the crew. I don't want my people to become tyrants in their own way and terrorize the systems. I want to unify them.

After all that are not on shift have gotten a go at the two men, I ask Brad to make sure they never become a problem anymore and to space them once we come out of jump space. I turn to Weil and see that she's barely touched the leader and he seems to be spilling his guts out. The recorder is on so I will be able to hear everything back later. I incline my head a bit toward the men and Weil simply nods toward the two men being dragged out of the room. It seems seeing his friends beaten by the rest of the crew was incentive enough to loosen his tongue.

I leave the room and head to my room, the mountain of rock now behind me again. Once we're out of earshot of anyone else, I ask him to move next to me.

"Commander, the Captain might like to spend a bit more time with you."

"I told the captain that I could not leave your side anymore because of what happened. None of this would have happened had I stayed by your side like my job requires."

"Commander, Hank, none of this is your fault. They were bound to find another time to try and hurt or kill me. I'm glad it happened at that moment as I had plenty of support from Diana. If this were to happen ground side, where civilians could be hurt, it would be much worse."

"Admiral, we cannot lose you."

"I'm just one person Commander, nothing special."

I see he's uncomfortable about something and stop in the corridor, look both ways, and try to look him in the eyes. Damn he's tall.

"What's going on Hank. Now don't Admiral me, or be all proper and polite. I want the plain truth, even if it hurts."

He looks both sides of the corridor and when a crew member walks our way, he looks at him with hard eyes and the man turns around and almost runs away.

"Admiral, there is a prophecy on my planet that an outsider will one day come and destroy the universe. That person will fight off the worst enemy the races have ever seen and will re-make the universe into one.

I'm giving you the simplified version, but in essence I believe that person is you, and I need to make sure you survive to fulfill your destiny."

"How can you be sure that this person is me?"

"I cannot explain it yet, but once we arrive at our second destination all will be clearer."

"And just where will our second destination be? I'm not even sure where we'll go from Glengarry."

Hank stops talking and resumes his post behind me a bit and looks forward. I start walking again and soon find myself in front of my hatch. I hesitate before opening the hatch but when I look back at my escort, he's silent and watchful. I enter my room and head straight for bed, not caring what time it is, and fall asleep in seconds.

6

Chapter 6

The rest of the trip is thankfully uneventful, and soon I forget what Hank told me and concentrate on the day to day of running a fleet of twenty-seven ships, soon to grow tenfold. I work with Geraldine to find buyers for the other companies I own, ones that not only will become assets in the future but are also deserving. I need good people that have a business sense and won't go nuts at the amount of money they will make and start spending it all and lose the business.

On Glengarry I have six businesses that are profitable but not to the point they could be. Alan might have had a sense to make money, but it was usually at the expense of someone else, someone like Angela Laurent.

Twelve years ago, Angela started a business in computer data pads that were faster, lighter and compatible with all systems used in the known systems. She was a small business owner and to expand into the market she needed to make serious money, she needed an investor. Unfortunately, she fell on Alan. He made her sign a contract that was created by his now defunct accountant and Angela soon after lost control of the company and not long after that was pushed aside by Alan himself.

Now Angela has a small business repairing computers or anything tech. She's about to become much wealthier than she ever had with Alan as a partner. Since Angela is Kroh, I will bring Diana to the meeting with me, and of course Hank will follow. He hasn't left my side since the incident, except when I enter my room. Brad has a guard posted there at all times, even when Hank is there.

I call Diana in for a briefing before we come out of jump space. There is something I need to know before I get into a meeting with another Kroh.

"I need to ask you something and I need a straight answer." I ask her as soon as she sits down. "Are all Kroh telepathic?"

She looks down at her hands before lifting her eyes to mine. "We are."

"And I'm guessing that no one outside of Kroh society knows this, not even the old Conranians."

"Correct."

"Good, let's keep it that way. Now we're going into a meeting with a Kroh that got swindled by Alan and I plan to repay her a hundred times for what he did to her. I want you in there with me."

"You don't want people to know of my ability, not even the rest of the guards?"

"Hell no! This is too precious a secret to put out into the world. Kroh will be hunted by assholes like Alan for their talents and used as slaves. I'll die before any of your kind is kept as slaves. Hell, I plan on eliminating slaves all together. My to-do list is growing quite large don't you think? I hope I live long enough to accomplish half of it."

"What happens when Angela learns of your knowledge?"

I smile because I never told her the name of the buyer, and now I see her blushing because she knows she slipped up. Better practice sweetie, you can't slip with the others.

"That's part of the reason I want you there. You'll need to convince her that I'm not a threat to your secret."

"That won't be a problem, Sherry."

The next morning comes and Elena lets me know we'll be out of jump space in two hours, so I have both Geraldine and Diana prepare their things and meet me in the situation room. Hank is already there and soon after Brad comes in.

"Admiral, I've prepared your escort for your trip into town ground side." Brad says.

"Escort Captain?"

"With the situation that happened on board, we cannot take any chances."

"And my goal is not to attract too much attention. That will be hard enough with three gorgeous women escorted by the largest walking mountain in the universe, an escort will surely make it impossible."

I smile at Hank so he knows I'm just kidding. I've grown to like his presence around me, the safety it brings. I don't know anyone alive that would go up against a Fernonian even with three to one odds, and if anyone is stupid enough to do so will not only have Hank to deal with but a bad ass Kroh and a Conranian that is just looking for a fight.

Diana cocks an eyebrow at me at the last comment.

'Sorry, but that fight showed me more possibilities my power gives me and I can't wait to try them out again.'

'Sure, and show the whole universe that the Conranians are back and bring the Vuldalians on us again. Also, it is not good to wish for a fight. Peace is a better solution unless peace is impossible, then you fight.'

'Fine. Party pooper.'

'What's a party pooper?'

I leave the question unanswered as Brad is waiting for an answer. What was his question again?

'He wants to know if he can at least post the guard to follow from a distance.'

"That will be fine Captain, but not too close."

'Thanks.'

'My pleasure, Admiral.'

'Don't you start calling me that into my head.'

Brad walks around the group going into the city and distributes ear pieces that will help us communicate between each other.

At the exact time Elena mentions that we're coming out of jump space the light show appears again on the main screen of the situation room. Soon after that we emerge into real space and find ourselves into oncoming traffic. None of it is close enough to be a danger but with twenty-seven ships coming out of jump space at the same time the scanning officer must be going crazy trying to advise his boss of an invasion. Elena sends the prepared message to the planetary authorities and we get out of the way of coming traffic to a prearranged point mentioned in the message.

Not long after the message arrived at their station a trio of attack ships comes our way at an attack pace. Elena warned me that they might try this tactic to see how we react. She orders all ships to stand at the ready but not to raise shields or she would blow them up herself. I had not mentioned that part, but I still agree with the warning. I need to be able to land on Glengarry unhindered otherwise we'll have trouble everywhere else we try to land.

All ships travel to the established location except for the two ships Kevin had warned me about. They accelerate toward the planet for a few seconds until the engines stop as quickly as they came on, and then slowly they turn around and come to their designated position. The comm to my chair flashes and I answer it, expecting Elena or Kevin, but find one of Rjoart's men looking at anything but me, his eyes menacing and deadly.

"Situation under control Admiral." He says, the body of the former Captain on the ground behind him, missing its head.

"Understood, thank you." Is all I say.

My guess from seeing Rjoart in action, the soldier assigned to the bridge was never seen by any of the people on it, and when the two captains decided to make their move, they lost their heads seconds after. The quick action of the two assassins made a very bad situation into a controllable one. There will be time enough to choose new Captains for those ships later as the attack ships arrive close to our position but far enough that they can evade weapon's fire if we're stupid enough to do so. The comm light flashes again and Elena answers it, as Captain of the lead ship and in charge of the fleet.

"This is Captain Elena Ross, Fleet Commander of The Red Widow Group aboard the *Red Widow*, how may I be of service today."

The smile on her face and in her voice just screams don't piss me off. The duo of ships breaking formation probably the source of her frustration.

"This is planetary control ship Delta. You got a problem with your Captains Fleet Commander?"

"Nope, problem is taken care of and will never be a problem

again."

The man on the other end of the comm actually gulps at the coldness in her voice in describing what he believes to be two dead Captains. He's right of course.

"The Council would like to know of your goals in entering the system in force."

"We have transactions to do, goods to purchase for the ships, and hopefully a little R&R if possible."

"For now, the Council has permitted a single shuttle to land at the spaceport and meet with them about the exact purpose of your visit."

"Like that's gonna happen pal. I will not allow one of my shuttles to leave the safety of my ship to travel all the way to the planet surface. My ship will travel back with you while the rest of my ships will stay at this exact location. If you've got a problem with that then try and stop me."

The anger in her eyes was real, but probably not due to the words the escort ship said.

"Fine, I will lead the way while my two counterparts will follow you. Is that acceptable?"

"That sounds peachy sweetheart. Lead on."

The comm cuts and Elena has the ship move forward slowly until it clears the other ships and then follows the attack ships at their speed, even forcing them to go a bit faster when they're going too slow for her taste.

"Captain Waxman has control of the Fleet while I'm gone." Elena announces on the Fleet frequency. "If anyone has a problem with that you can take it up with Commander Ionicci when we get back."

Well, that's a surprise. I trust Kevin not to betray us, but to leave him in charge of the Fleet could be a risky move. But I placed Elena in charge of the Fleet for a reason, and I need to trust her judgment on this.

We arrive in orbit around Glengarry and Elena has her second in command take charge and walks to join us in the cargo hold where two shuttles await us. Both look like regular civilian shuttles, but looks are deceiving in this matter, as Hector had them refitted with armor, a shield generator and a couple of ship size blasters. Of course, they would not be able to sustain much damage before the shuttle is destroyed, but the goal is to give the occupants a chance to escape by surviving the initial attack.

I enter one of the shuttles with Geraldine, Diana, Hank and Brad, while the rest of the guard accompany Elena and another security officer aboard the other. Once on the ground the guards with Elena would spread out and when out of sight of anyone would make their way to follow me and my entourage. I hate to leave Elena with only one security officer but there was nothing for it. I argued long and hard with Brad about keeping a few more with my Captain but even she argued against it.

The flight into the atmosphere is uneventful except for the usual turbulence I'm told always happens when entering a planet's air supply. As we land a large group of soldiers run our way, all in formation, and stop close to our shuttles and come to attention. A single man walks up to the shuttles as the hatches open. He's dressed in military fatigues, armed with a hand blaster and holds himself perfectly straight in spite of the thinning white hair on his head. He walks to Elena and stops at attention but does not salute. He knows she's not military, yet.

"Captain Ross, I am Major Ben Stock Jr of the Glengarry

military. Welcome to our planet. You were told a single shuttle was to enter our atmosphere. Can I ask why you defy our arrangement?"

As arranged on the way here, I'm the one that comes forward and play the role I hate playing but it is necessary.

"I'm sorry sir, it's my fault. I've never been here before I could not pass the chance to visit and shop. Your planet seems so beautiful from space that I had to come and see from the ground. I won't be any trouble I promise. Can I stay please?"

I use my 'I'm pretty but stupid' voice and 'look in my beautiful eyes' look hoping the Major will not ask us to go back.

'You do act pretty well in that role Sherry.'

'You do know I can punish you by making you clean the latrines on the ship.'

'I've done worse in my youth.'

'I can tell that man at the mess hall that you would love to go on a date with him.'

'overcautious I'll stop.'

"I guess if you can promise not to make any trouble and make sure your large friend there doesn't get into any fights."

"Who Hank, he's harmless."

"Miss, I've known several Fernonians in my lifetime and none of them are harmless. And Hank here looks more dangerous than all of them combined. No offense sir."

"None taken Major." Hank replies.

"Fine you may shop in the city but I ask that you do not venture outside of the main city."

"Oh, thank you so much sir, we promise we won't."

I leave with Hank, Geraldine and Diana while the Major talks to the rest of the group. I trust Elena to take care of business at the port authorities. She has the list of what each ship needs and has access to an account set up by Geraldine with enough to buy a brand-new ship with. She should have enough for parts and food.

Diana leads the way out of the spaceport and turns off the main street right away toward the poorer side of the main city. I can already feel Hank tensing as we enter shady streets and shadier people watch us go by. On the comm I hear Hank ask Brad for back up as soon as possible, but with Diana there and I'm no slouch I do have to admit, we should be fine. I don't hear any response from Brad but that doesn't mean anything, and he might be too busy to reply.

Some of the people on the streets make a move to walk toward us until Hank clears his throat and they finally notice him and run away faster than if the police were after them. For now, he scares them enough to prevent an assault, but they might gang up on us and outnumber us.

'We're almost there.' Diana says into my mind.

'Why not say it out loud?'

'Because I don't want Hank to relax his stance. Right now, he's the only reason the large group behind us hasn't attacked.'

'I didn't realize there were people behind us.'

'They follow from the next street, waiting for the right moment to attack. They won't get it. We're here.'

Diana turns into a small store without a sign and turns to Hank.

"Wait outside, otherwise we might bring trouble to the shop owner."

"And if they ambush us before we can get out?"

Hank was not scared; he was just asking a simple question. Simple and quiet. I'm not sure he ever gets scared.

"Then we'll cut our way out of here."

Diana could sound as deadly as Hank sometimes. I'm so happy the guards are on my side and not against me. Inside the shop are a few electronic items, nothing too fancy, but all looks to be in pristine condition even if it dates back fifty years. Angela seems like the right person for the job, if I can convince her to take it.

A small woman of about fifty steps out of the back room and walks toward the small counter she keeps to place something between the customers and herself. Bright woman. I approach her and begin in Kroh.

"Good day Wise one, I wish to talk to you about your past but especially your future."

Then I talk to her in my mind.

'I know you are reading my thoughts so you know who I am and why I am here. My husband is dead, thank whatever God you believe in, and I now have sole ownership of all his assets. He stole something from you in the past and used his influence to block your project so he and his friends could continue to control the population. I am here to end that control and restore you to the place in history you should have had all along.'

"I am not interested in what a Conranian has to say." She starts in Kroh. "I do not know how you learned of our ability," she looks at Diana, "but I will not work for one of the Great Ones that betrayed this universe and failed us all those years ago."

"She is not like those of the past, she has a different mindset." Diana pitches in.

"My goal is not for you to work for me. I want to give you the companies, all of them on Glengarry. I only ask a very small percentage of the profits, and that profit will be used to purchase some of the items I will need to protect the systems from any threat coming for us."

"And what's in it for me, eternal servitude? Will I have to do as you ask like the deal you made with Fuentez?"

"No, nothing like his. I have it right here."

I gesture toward Geraldine to give me the pad and hand it over to Angela. She looks at it and then goes to switch pages to read the rest, but nothing happened.

"Where's the rest of the agreement?"

"What rest are you talking about?" I ask.

"All the fine print, all the if this, if that, that we always find in contracts."

"There are none. That is the full contract. The companies are yours, period. Whatever I will ask of you will be as a customer. In essence the ten percent commission comes with no strings attached. I do not decide what you do, how you spend the money, nothing. I hire you to make something like any other customer would. Your past has proven that you are a very intelligent woman with a good heart. You've seen my mind, how I think. Do you think you would fit well with my organization?"

"I do, but I like the no strings attached clause. I can finally create the system I wanted to implement."

"And it will be my honor to distribute it for you once it is finished, at an excellent discount as well. I have the same goals you have, that all races work together once and for all. It will be essential in the years to come I believe."

"Trouble coming." Comes the notice from Brad.

"Angela, I have to go as I'm afraid our group has brought trouble to your location, I am very sorry. If you would like to, we could all leave together and visit your new companies together."

"Now?"

"I don't see why we need to delay, do you? All you need to do is sign with your print, I will do the same, and Geraldine will process all the necessary documents while we drive there."

Angela turns to Diana and I know they are having a mental conversation. Angela finally places her thumb to the pad and then I place mine next to hers. I give it back to Geraldine and Angela runs to the back and grabs a bag and a jacket.

"Let's go." She says.

"What about your things, the gear?" I ask.

"There is nothing here of real value, so the looters won't find it to their liking. I have more important things in my bag."

We step outside and Hank is staring down at least twenty guys with a variety of hand weapons, like clubs, chains and anything else they could grab at a moment's notice. I'm sure Hank could take them all, but my goal is not to get into trouble, so I slowly walk in front of Hank and look the men straight in the eyes, each one of them. I slowly raise the power inside me and have blue electricity surround my hands. All back up a bit, still not afraid enough to leave a potential good score. One of the bravest or stupidest comes forward with speed. He flies back over his buddies as my hand hits his chest. That does the trick.

All of them run for their lives and scream of a witch. Not stealthy at all, but effective. I turn to the others and Angela's eyes are wide as saucers and closes her mouth as I look her way.

"Shall we go?" I ask and start walking toward the main street to grab a cab.

We walk in a group and soon are joined by the rest of

the guard, Angela looking at them strangely but not saying anything as we don't.

'If you wanted to stir up shit all over the planet, that was a good way to do it.'

'Relax Diana, what's the worst that could happen?'

'The enemy find's out you exist and come crashing down on us.'

'She's right Sherry-Ann. I may call you Sherry-Ann?'

'Yes, you may Angela. And will the both of you relax. I have a plan and all is going well. By the time the Vuldalians are here, if they come, we'll be more than ready for them.'

"Brad, walk with me, will you?" I ask.

He walks up to me and looks at me funny.

"What?"

"Why did you use your power back there? We had them all covered."

"I don't doubt it, but time is of the essence. The Major at the spaceport, I'd like him to join our group. We'll need more than one leader in the Marines and since your main job is to protect me, I need someone with experience to lead the force I'm building."

"What force? We have less than fifty men and women spread out on twenty-seven ships."

"The Red Marines will be equipped like none other before them, all with the help of Angela's new companies, and the minerals I asked Alvaro to collect."

"I'm pretty sure you're all making this up as you go."

"I am, but I'm guided by the power inside me."

"And what do I offer your Major to entice him to leave the Glengarry military to join the Red Marines?"

"Whatever it takes. Bring Geraldine with you."

81

"Why me?" she asks.

"Because you'll be able to draw up the contracts for him and whatever men he brings with him. Go now before his shift finishes."

Both share a look, one that only siblings shared and knew the meaning to.

'What exactly will I be helping you build?'

'Battle armor suits. The material I'm having Alvaro set aside is essential to making these armor suits impervious to blaster fire as well as be flexible enough for the men and women to move freely in them. You will supply the electronics for the suit. I will purchase them of course.'

'How many suits do you plan on making?'

'At least ten thousand, but a hundred thousand would be best before the enemy shows up.'

Angela misses a step and Hector quickly catches her before she falls to the ground.

'I think he likes you, Angela. He keeps looking your way.'

'Probably to make sure I don't fall on my face.'

'Look into his mind for a second and tell me I'm wrong.'

A few seconds go by and still no word from Angela.

'So, am I wrong?'

'None of your business.'

I smile and reach the main road and quickly find a cab large enough for all to fit inside. The ride to the head office of the Glengarry operations is a small drive away and I get to see the sights, which are not that great in the city. I wish we could leave for a few days and visit the first planet other than Alexandria I've ever gone on, but first we need to get down to business so Angela can have her operation up and running.

Alan had only been making products that have a short expiry

life, like all his other billionaire friends, but that needs to end now. With what I feel is coming soon, the Alliance will need better gear, better ships and yes, probably better management. The craze about having more and more money needs to leave and be replaced by the need to better humanity and its allies.

The Alliance has over a hundred member systems, but a lot of them are separate states only in the Alliance for the protection. Most of these do not participate actively in the affairs of everyday life, and that needs to change.

'Yes Angela, that also means the Kroh system.'

'And how do you plan on getting them to accept your plan?'

'I have no clue as of yet, but something will come up sooner or later.'

"Admiral, radio chatter is saying that a large force is gathering around our destination. Armed personnel are on site but not to disperse the trouble makers, but to join them. It seems they are supporters of your late husband."

"Thank you, Commander. Captain Sillens, did you hear the message from Commander Ionicci?"

"I did Admiral. What are your plans? Do you need me to come join you?"

"I don't think one extra person would do much of a difference Captain. If you had an army with you that might be a different matter, but even though your skills are incredible, you are just one man."

And there it is, the seeds planted for Brad to get the army I need, and the Major to lead it. A desperate Brad can do anything. Now, how to handle the crowd until he gets it?

'I might be able to help in that Admiral.' Angela says.

"Angela, do you have any ideas on how to handle these men at your new company?" I ask out loud.

83

"I believe I might have something in mind, but it might still involve some bloodshed."

"Some bloodshed is better than a complete massacre."

"You believe they would kill us all?"

"No."

"Oh. Your power, you can do other stuff than just push people far away, can you?"

"I can. Hector, guard Angela with your life. She's pivotal in my upcoming plans. Diana, Julie, Aaron and Weil, I want the instigators of this riot against their rightful owner to stop."

"They might not like you for what they believe you did to their boss." Aaron says.

"That might be Aaron, but I'm not the owner of the companies, Angela is. So, they're rebelling against one of their own, the person that created the initial company. I want the instigators because those are Alan's men through and through."

"How about your protection Admiral?"

"Commander Ionicci would not leave my side even if I forced him to. He's protection enough guys."

The cab stops a little way off the grounds to the main building of the companies and we all get out. Right away the four guards that are tasked with finding the instigators run off in different directions while Hank, Angela, Hector and I walk slowly toward the riot starting in the front of the entrance to the main company building. As soon as we're close enough for the first rioters to see us a group of ten take off and run toward us. One stays back and starts yelling to the rest of the people that we've arrived but his words are cut short by a single blaster bolt to the head.

"One down." Julie says.

People around the downed agitator look around scared, but

not many flee. Good, I want them here for the final act. The ten men approach a little too close for Hank's taste so he gives Hector a look and rushes the men. Hector places himself in front of us and looks around to make sure no one becomes a threat.

The men falter a bit when they see Hank rush them, but believe their numbers will give them an advantage. They don't know many Fernonians that's for sure. Hank gets to the men and swings his right arm. Two men fly off several meters in the air and land on the ground immobile. His left arm does the same with the same effect. Now the six men left hesitate, but it's too late as Hank pounds one on the head. The three remaining hit Hank at the same time, but the almost eight feet mountain of rock and muscle doesn't even feel it and sends one spinning away with an uppercut, another with a backward slap to the chest and the last he catches before the man can run away only to throw him high up into a tree where he lies either unconscious or immobile for fear Hank will down the tree only to get back to hitting him.

"Two down." Weil says.

I didn't hear the crack of a blaster but then I was busy looking at my bodyguard pounding idiots all over the grounds.

"Three down." Diana says.

"Four and five down." Aaron says almost on top of her.

"That's all we can find Admiral." Weil says.

"Excellent guard, nice work. Angela, now's your turn. Do what you have to do."

She walks a little faster to get to the people before I do, Hector by her side. Hank now by mine I do not feel the need to draw on my power. Angela gets close to the crowd and attracts the attention of someone. The middle-aged man sees her and at first doesn't seem to remember her, but soon his eyes go big as does his smile. He runs toward her and Hector places himself in front of Angela for protection. She places a gentle hand on his arm and he lets the man pass. By now I'm close enough to hear their words.

"Angela, I thought you were dead."

"That's for another time Oliver. What's going on?"

"The people are rebelling against the owner of the company. McDonald was really bad, but they say the woman that had him killed to take over the company is a witch and will turn us into slaves."

"I'm not sure who they are, but they're full of shit. First, the woman you're referring to is not a witch, on the contrary, she's kind and considerate. Second, she didn't have her husband killed, he died in a ship explosion. Third, she doesn't own this company or all the others on Glengarry, I do."

She lifts the pad copy that Geraldine had given her as proof of the sale and shows Oliver. His eyes go wide as he looks back at her.

"This is a trap of some kind Angela, same as the first time."

"Oliver, do you think me such a fool as to fall for the same trick twice? Look at the fine print on the contract?"

"What fine print, I can't see any."

"Exactly. This woman's only goal is for me to finish what I started all those years ago, and to finish it under my conditions and with my desires. And she didn't only give me my company back, she gave me all the Glengarry operations. I own everything Alan McDonald owned, and it didn't cost me a credit. All she asked of me is to finish the work I started all those years ago and never got to finish."

"But why? Everyone has an angle. She must have something

up her sleeve."

"I do mister Oliver. That something is for Angela to help all the races communicate better between them and work together." I say as I approach the two.

"Oliver, meet Admiral Sherry-Ann Lebronski, widow of McDonald and the former owner of this place."

Oliver looks at me and then at Hank, fear in his eyes. Now Angela goes in for the kill.

"Oliver, you have two choices now. Back when that scum took my company away from me you stayed because he made you a deal and I understand why you did it. That amount of money is hard to resist. Now I give you a choice of my own. Either you help me stop this right now and we can start working on something meaningful, or you continue to think this woman is a witch and I ask Hector here to stop the riot starting with you? What will it be?"

Oliver looks sideways at Hector and his decision comes out in the form of grabbing his comm unit and contacting someone inside the building.

"Alex, time for this to end. Send out the guards and arrest the ones that continue. I want this place back to work in twenty or I'll have your head."

"Yes sir." Comes the reply over the comm.

"Welcome back boss." He says as he walks back toward the people rioting.

A small commotion comes from behind as hover tanks and other armored vehicles arrive, at the head of them are Brad and Major Stock. The sight of the military moves people faster than Oliver asked and in less than five minutes the ground is clear of protesters except for the five bodies the guard took out. Without the leaders of the riot the rest were easy to convince.

Brad and Ben walk up to me with sad looks in their eyes.

"Captain Sillens here promised me a fight to remember. I don't see much of a fight at all." The Major says.

"Major, you'll have your fight soon enough, just not on this planet. How many men have you hired Captain Sillens?"

Ben is the one to answer.

"All of my platoon Admiral. Nice acting at the port by the way."

"Thank you Major, both for your men and for the compliment."

"The captain here tells me you're Conranian. Didn't even know there were still some of you out there. Do you plan on ruling the galaxy like your predecessors or just going around from planet to planet hiring military people?"

"I haven't given ruling much thought yet, but I will hire every good outfit of soldiers I can to make sure we defeat the enemy that is coming. If we survive the large fight coming, I'll think about ruling if I see myself fit for that duty."

'Angela, do you need anything else from me?'

'I will need the plans to what you will need for those suits you want.'

'It's all in the pad you have in your hands. My contact info is also on there so you can contact me when you've figured it out.'

'What about Hector?'

"Hector, I believe Angela will need someone she can trust to protect her, and I would greatly appreciate it if that person was you. Call it a temporary assignment for the guard."

Hector nods my way and gives me a small smile of thanks. I look toward Aaron.

"Aaron, I know you and Hector are close friends. If you wish to stay as well you can. He will need all the help he can get setting up a proper security force for the company."

"Nah, he's a pain in my ass most of the time. Besides, you'd miss my cooking too much."

"That I would Aaron, that I would."

I walk slowly next to him to whisper in his ear.

"I can order you to stay the same as Hector. You wouldn't lose face and you'd be a great asset to Angela."

"Thank you for the thought Admiral, but I'd rather stick with you for now. Maybe later."

I nod and we head out to the hover tanks and other military vehicles. I'll need to contact a couple more ships to transport my new army's vehicles and personnel. Then I have a thought.

"Hector, you still on comms?"

"I am Admiral."

"Which ship would you…"

"The *Hand of God* would be my choice for the platoon Admiral. It has the cargo space, lots of extra quarters and they could probably build themselves a training area in it. Excellent armor and shields to keep them safe. Oh, and it can enter a planet's atmosphere unlike some of your ships."

"How did you know I would ask you that Hector?"

"In the small time I've been with you Sherry, I've learned to think ahead four steps otherwise I'm behind on what you need. Julie will be able to replace me in this. Her knowledge of ships is almost equal to my own. Be safe Sherry, I plan on seeing you again soon."

"Thank you, Hector, for all you did. Be safe as well and take care of Angela."

The ride to the spaceport is a quick one as the military vehicles make short work of the many kilometers separating

Angela's company to the port pad. There we find Elena talking heatedly with the port manager I'm told by Ben. I can't wait to see what this is all about.

As all the military vehicle land next to our two shuttles the port manager goes white at the site of Major Stock walking next to me. I don't get a chance to speak as the Major walks a bit faster and settles himself right in front of the manager, making the smaller man look up at him.

"Problem Albert?" he says simply.

"Yes Ben. This woman is trying to bring in all of her ships close to the planet and even wants to land one at the spaceport."

"And?"

I look at Brad and he nods, letting me know he sent word to Elena about the platoon needing transport. The other part is probably having to do with the multiple food trucks and munitions vehicles coming in and lining up toward our shuttles. It seems Elena's been spending my money. Good. If she believes that we need everything that's in those trucks than we do.

"Well…" the manager tries to complain, but the larger man squares his shoulders and the manager cuts off.

"The people following Admiral Lebronski are not here to cause trouble Albert. If I look at the amount of vehicles lined up and the ones still trying to enter the port, I'd say they're helping the economy quite a bit. And, if I judge by the good heart of the Admiral, she would be willing to pay a one percent tax fee for you to permit her ships to land in priority so we can get out of here faster. Am I right Admiral?"

This costs me a huge chuck of money extra, but the time saved will be well worth it in the long run. I nod to Albert and Ben.

Ben has his men move out and secure a large portion of the spaceport for our ships to land before Albert can complain and the rest of my team moves back to our shuttle. Elena follows as does Ben.

"Elena, I'll leave the finer details to you as I move back to the ship. I'll leave some of the guard with you…"

Ben clears his throat.

"Begging your pardon Admiral, but ground security of the crew is my job now, not that of your personal guard. They are extremely capable, but they need to be doing their job, which is protecting you. I'll take care of the security of the products as well as moving things along at a faster pace. We'll have this stuff loaded in half the time."

"Excellent Major. Thank you. Is that good with you Captain?"

"That's more than good Admiral. Come on Major, let's kick these truckers into high gear. I'll call the ships right away."

By the time our shuttle enters the loading bay of our ship most of the ships are halfway to the planet and we see two larger cargo shuttles enter the atmosphere for the *Red Widow*. Twenty-six hours later all the ships have been replenished in food, ammunition, and our first Army Platoon is aboard its very own ship. The Captain of the *Hand of God*, Paul Voisin, happens to be an ex-marine soldier injured in combat and learned to pilot ships after that. He came up in ranks aboard a civilian freighter but when Brad came to see him about a job on a warship, he never hesitated.

Although in history there is a rivalry between navy and army, both are still the same types of soldiers, just on different fields of battle. My goal would be to have a force that could change from one to the other and be effective both on ship operations as well as on the ground. That would permit me to be more versatile when the enemy showed up. It would be good to know who this enemy is and what types of weaponry they have. But I keep telling myself that I have to take one thing at a time. These memories and ideas popping into my head have started going at light speed and I find that everything is going too slow.

Time to leave this system and head for the next target. Not far from Glengarry is Peace, a colony that was established mainly by Canadian colonists that wish to have a world of their own that would be in their image. They accept people from all nations, race and religion, but you need to want to live in peace otherwise they will throw you off the planet faster than you can say poutine. That's a French-Canadian delicacy back on Earth that my memories tell me is fabulous for the taste buds but murder on the diet. Can't wait to try it.

Julie comes from that system and if I can convince them to join my cause I will not only have a great friendly partner, but an incredible ally on the battlefield. Like my guard, the state that wants peace will protect it at all cost, and if you come to harm anyone of their friends, you'll pay dearly for the insult.

In our absence Kevin placed a new command crew on each of the offending ship back when we entered Glengarry. I believe we can trust the crew will be well watched, enough so that I recalled my own Rjoart and his team of assassins. He brings them aboard the *Red Widow* so that I can meet each of them. Elena has made Kevin her second in command of the Fleet and although I would think some grumbling would happen given where he comes from, none come to my ears so I let Elena deal with it.

Midway to our destination I'm sitting in the situation room

going through files I have on Peace so that I can prepare myself for a meeting with their leaders. This will be the first stop I make where Alan did not have any companies but it doesn't mean I do not want to invest in the place. They have extensive medical facilities that almost rival the ones found on the Brandari home world. That could become an excellent choice to invest in healthcare and get them to branch out onto other worlds making all of the Alliance safe and well cared for.

I'm amerced fully into a medical file that I would normally understand nothing of if not for the memories inside me when the general alarm sounds. What now?

"Admiral," Elena comes on my screen, "Fernon is under attacked."

7

Chapter 7

"We just got a request for help broadcasts in all directions. If the Fernonians are asking for help Admiral it means the situation is really bad."

"Then what are you waiting for, change course and let's give them the help we can. How long until we get there?"

"Ten minutes Admiral, we're basically in their front yard already."

"Alert all ships to be battle ready the second we come out of jump space."

"Yes ma'am."

"Commander, assemble the guard and get them to the attack shuttle. That's an order." I add as he's about to refuse so he doesn't leave me. "I'll join you in a minute."

"Admiral, you cannot risk yourself on the planet in the middle of a large-scale attack." He replies at the door.

"Watch me." I snap then turn to the comms.

"Major Stock, looks like you'll get your big battle sooner than I thought. We're heading to Fernon and we head ground side the second we enter normal space."

"We Admiral?"

"Hell yes we. Now get your men ready."

I switch channels again.

"Captain Voisin, the second you hit normal space punch it for the planet. I want the troops on the ground no more than ten minutes after we appear in system."

"Roger that ma'am."

I keep switching frequencies.

"Captain Ross, I need the smugglers for the ground assault. You have command of the rest of the ships. Give them hell for me."

"Got it Admiral. They won't know what hit them."

And for the last comm frequency before leaving the situation room.

"Captain Williams, I need your four ships for the ground assault. You guys have tricks no one else has seen. We might need a minor miracle to get us safely on the ground, you're it."

"We won't let you down Admiral."

As soon as the comm cuts I get up and look at the rest of the crew in the situation room, all looking at me. I hope this won't be the last I see of them.

"Give them hell guys."

I run off toward the cargo bay and arrive to find the rest of the guard, Hank, and all of the assassins waiting for me. Well, if this crew can't install fear into an enemy, then they don't know what fear is.

No one wastes any time and we get into two attack shuttles and wait for the signal that we're back in normal space. We'll have to hide behind the larger ships as our shuttles are not equipped for too much damage, but with the large *Hand of God* and the four smaller ships flying close together, we should be able to evade enemy detection.

The signal finally comes and off we go. The shuttle darts off much faster than I thought possible for a ship this small. Our pilot takes us into maneuvers that would make my stomach empty itself if I had eaten just before the alarm. Thankfully the harness securing me to the seat is tight and I can't move. The screen in front changes to the scene of the battle raging on outside, and it is terrifying. I may have brought my full fleet to its doom, but I cannot let someone hurt another planet I wish to befriend. I can't recognize the ships attacking Fernon even with the memories inside me, so this is a new foe. My ships are taking a beating but I'm happy to say their giving at least as much in return.

Soon we start hitting the atmosphere and none of the enemy ships have targeted us. That's good but it also means they do not believe we're that much of a threat to the force on the ground. Their bad.

"Pilot, get me a line to the Fernon command."

A few seconds later I get a rough voice similar to Hank's.

"What do you want Human, we're busy?"

"Nice to see you too. Where's the worst of the fighting? I've got a large force that can help."

"At what cost? No thank you, we're not interested in your help."

All of a sudden Hank gets on the line with a tone I've never heard before.

"This is Prince Hank Ionicci the third. You will tell us where the fighting is worst so we may assist or I swear when I get off this ship, I'll skin you alive in front of your kids and then leave you in the middle of the ocean!"

Did he say Prince?

"I'm sorry my Prince, I was unaware you were with the force coming in. The Palace is being overrun sir. That would be the best possible option to help."

"Your name and position?" Hank asks.

"Decker sir, planetary communications."

"You better hope that my parents are still alive Decker."

He cuts the comm and looks at all of us.

"What?"

No one dares say anything to him and we all prepare to get off as the shuttle banks hard to the right. Not long after that the pilot announces ten seconds before disembarking. The brakes on this shuttle would make most sports hovercars jealous and I thank again the person that equipped the shuttle with excellent straps.

The cargo hatch opens and I can see blaster bolts flying by the hatch but none of us hesitate. The second shuttle is right next to us and Rjoart's team are out and ready for action. The Major's hover tanks are out before the ship comes fully to the ground, the armor taking a beating on the ship. All of a sudden four ships fly overhead and explosions can be heard where most of the fire to the ship had been coming from. None hit the ship after the run.

"Major, get your men to secure the outside of the Palace and take down anything not on our side. We're heading inside. Captain Williams, keep the *Hand of God* safe and enemy free. I'm counting on you."

I don't wait for a response and we head for the stairs to the Palace a few hundred yards away. The way is blocked by hundreds of enemy soldiers firing at the Fernonians protecting the Palace. I've never really seen Hank mad, but I believe he's far off mad now and going toward death walking as he takes the lead and uses a staff I've never seen him have before and he goes hunting for enemy. The guard and assassins make a line and we simply destroy anything in our path.

I don't have time to look at what the others are doing as the enemy now knows we're here and turn toward us. The power inside flares up like never and I send bolts of electricity at all enemy I see in my path. None of them get too close except for one who jumps over the rest of my attacks but just as he comes close to landing on me a rock crashes into him and tears him in two. I look toward my left and see Hank grabbing his staff from the air where he threw it so he could grab a rock. I nod while still throwing bolt after devastating bolt toward the enemy. I can see Rjoart and his team far ahead as their swords deflect blaster bolts and direct them at other enemy attackers. Others fall to their deadly blades and soon the ground is littered with bodies of the dead.

We reach the top of the stairs and the guard turn to prevent any other enemy from coming up and threatening Hank's parents. But soon and smaller Fernonian comes out of the Palace and sees Hank and bows. Hank grabs his arm and lifts him.

"No time for formality. What's the situation inside?"

"Sir, we have bands of these enemy foes all over the Palace."

Hank looks at me and turns to Brad who nods.

"Protect her with your life."

"I will. Commander, take Rjoart and his team."

"I would be honored to have them."

Rjoart nods to Hank and starts moving forward but the other Fernonian comes in front of them.

"Sir, it would be sacrilege to have this filth inside the King's Palace."

"That filth you mention is my friend and so are the rest of his team. If you have a problem with them entering the Palace with me then I will take you out as well."

The rage in Hank's voice and eyes is beyond what I would have thought possible. The man wisely moves aside and Hank leads his assassin team inside.

I take the short reprieve to look at the situation and find that Ben's soldiers are taking out the enemy soldiers quickly with their vehicles and even prevent a few shuttles from leaving the scene. I decide to contact Elena and see how things are going up there.

"Elena, how are you doing?"

"Admiral, its Kevin. We're taking a beating but there ships are now coming apart at our concentrated fire."

"Kevin, what's happened to Elena?"

"Nothing major, just comms down from a major blast they took. The secondary team in the situation room are keeping me apprised of her situation. I have temporary command of the fleet due to her not being able to communicate orders."

"Excellent, keep up the good work."

No use asking about casualties at the moment. They need to concentrate on the fight. Suddenly Nathan Williams comes on the line.

"Admiral, you've got the mother of all comets heading straight for the Palace. They sent one of their badly damaged ships your way."

"Put everything you've got into that ships Nathan, I need it destroyed!"

He responds by having his four ships fly high to intercept the damaged ship. Missile after missile come out of the tubes, Gauss rifle slugs as well as every blaster he has, be it ship size or for fighters, fire a constant stream toward that ship. Explosion after explosion rock the enemy ship but a large chunk of it keeps heading our way. They won't do much to change its course now that it's in the atmosphere so we need to find something else. Then a burning sensation comes inside me.

The power accumulates inside, and it feels like it will burst every vein, shred my skin off my bones and shatter those very bones into a million pieces and still the power grows. Then I feel the moment for release is there and I spread my arms out toward the ship. An enormous cone shape ray of power explodes out of me and toward the enemy ship. And then darkness takes hold of me.

*****

Pain, that's all I feel as my eyes slowly open and blinding light assaults them. A few seconds later I realize I'm not back at the apartment after one of Alan's beatings, but... I don't know where I am really, but I do know I'm alive. My eyes adjust to the daylight coming through the window and I can see a landscape I've never seen before. A battered landscape with burnt trees and scorched earth. What a shame to do that to beings that never asked for war.

I hear a door open and slowly turn my head toward the sound only to find my field of view blocked by a wall of rocks. Is all their decoration also made of rocks? Then I realize that Hank is the one blocking my view. He hears me move and turns toward me.

"Admiral, are you OK?"

"Not sure yet Hank. Were you able to protect your family? How's the Palace?"

"The prince and his 'friends' were able to save us Admiral, and the Palace is as good as can be expected after an attack, thanks to you."

"Admiral, these are my parents the King and Queen of Fernon."

"Honored to meet you. The Commander has never spoken about you so I do not know your names. My name is Sherry-Ann Lebronski."

"The prince has mentioned your tendency for personal connection with the people you lead. This is uncommon on our world. It is also uncommon among Conranians if I remember correctly."

"I tend not to be conventional. Hank, how long have I been out?"

I see both the King and Queen shiver at the mention of their son's first name, but Hank doesn't even blink.

"Almost a week Admiral. In that time the fleet…" he never finishes as a commotion starts outside the door before a large crowd walks in.

The guard would not be left outside when their commander just wakes up after a week. The all nod to the King and Queen, and then surround the bed.

"About time you wake up Sherry, you missed the final battle?" Aaron says in his booming voice.

"The planet's been completely cleared of vermin and we're assisting with rebuilding the most important structures around the Capital." Says Ben.

"The fleet kicked ass Sherry, it was incredible to see." Elena adds, then turn to someone I do not know when she clears her throat. "Yeah, yeah, I'll present you. Sherry, this is Captain Hailey Jackson. She's part of a delegation of ten ships that showed up toward the end. Their appearance saved a lot of people on our ships and prevented the enemy from having any of their ships to escape."

"Thank you, Captain Jackson." I say. Damn, she's as gorgeous as Julie. Are all the people from that planet that beautiful?

'Yes, they are Sherry. It's frustrating.' Diana says in my mind.

The King and Queen seem shocked by the display of famil-iarity among the group. Too bad, I like it that way. Hank clears his throat and the others turn toward him. His parents also turn to him and I can see a glimmer of hope that someone will have the decency to act appropriately.

"As I was saying Sherry before they interrupted," Hank's parents almost faint at the first time he uses my first name, "the Fleet's almost finished with repairs and we should be ready to continue on our previous course."

"Excellent everyone. I'd like a moment alone with my personal bodyguard."

Everyone leaves except Hank's parents, who probably mean to follow him out the door, but when they realize the body-guard is him, they storm out in anger as he looks at them, waiting for them to leave also.

"That will be the only time you hear me say your first name Admiral."

"I know you did it to piss off your parents."

"When I left several years ago, they told me that I would never be able to return as part of the Royal family, so I never did. You saw this week how they mistrust the other races so for me to come back not only as the prince but with several different races and we end up saving the planet. They must be raging by now and that is what I wanted whenever I came back. Their belief that Fernonians are superior is absurd. Yes, we are a formidable force, but I would not have been able to clear the Palace without the help of Rjoart and his team.

The reason I stick to you so closely is that you draw in people of exception. This could be due to your ancestry, but I believe it has more to do with your way of trusting people and believing that they can do great things. For that I have pledged my life to protect yours. That is a far greater fate then leading a system that can't admit they need outside help."

"I'm glad you feel that way about me Hank, because I also feel the same about you and everyone else on the guard. Even if you would all disagree, I would give my life for any of you. Now can we get out of this place so I can see the rest of my fleet and its soldiers?"

He leads the way staying close at hand in case I find myself not steady on my feet. The effect of the blast of power seems to have worn off leaving behind an emptiness I cannot explain. Out of the hospital close to the Palace I see the end result to the battle that took place a week ago. But that is not the only result of this battle.

Although Hank's parents do not want to admit it, they do need help, now more than ever since their fleet has dwindled down to alarming levels. It seems that help is exactly what they have. Not only is my fleet in orbit and protecting the system as it gets repaired, but Captain Jackson's fleet of ten ships and another fifteen ships from different sectors have shown up in the system after hearing the distress call. Unlike the King and Queen, the population of Fernon look happy about the different races here to help protect them. I can even see several Fernonians talking with Rjoart and his team and laughing together. From what I saw during the attack, it seemed bad blood was between the two races.

Hank sees me looking at the happy scene and smiles.

"It seems the incredible heroics that the Xirtans showed in

the Palace and outside during the attack proved that they can be welcomed friends, and a lot of people have been talking to them to learn a bit more about them. That group over there now has been with them most of the day and they laugh regularly and seem to be getting along really well."

"At least some good has come of this tragedy."

Elena walks toward them with nonchalance and I know she wants some time alone with Hank. I excuse myself and walk to Rjoart and the large group together. The laughter dies down as I approach and that saddens me. I want them to be happy when they see me, not closed in.

To my surprise it is one of the Fernonians that speaks first.

"Admiral Lebronski, let me first thank you for saving us a week ago."

"I was far from alone. The people in my fleet make me look good."

"Your fleet is impressive as are your soldiers that came on the ground. That is why my friends and I wish to join your fleet. We will do any job you ask. All that we want is to help people as you do."

"Well, that is a surprise, but a very welcome one. Now I do not wish to insult you, quite the contrary, but since I have not been around Fernonians except Commander Ionicci, I cannot tell age, and I do not wish to accept your offer without making sure you are adults. I hope I did not misstep?"

"They are all of age Admiral," a woman says walking over, "except the two in the back there."

The two in question look ashamed that they have been discovered.

"But I give them permission to join your fleet if you so wish. The only favor I ask is that they are not to go out to fight on other planets until they become of age in five months."

"That is not a problem at all ma'am. We have plenty of positions to fill on the ships themselves, and with their strength I believe they could be of great help to the engineering department. As for the rest, you may not be accepted into the Marine Corps or the Army right away. There is much more to fighting than just hitting people with blasters. You will be given aptitude tests to be able to position you to best help the fleet. Is that acceptable for you all?"

All nod vigorously and I ask Rjoart to show them to the shuttles after they have gathered their belongings. The next few hours flies by as everyone wants their time with me and soon Elena walks slowly toward me and rescues me from a very boring conversation with diplomats from the Palace.

As we say goodbye to new friends, it is time to welcome the new group of trainees that have decided to join us.

"Elena, you seem disturbed. Everything good between you and Hank?"

"Oh yes, that's actually going great. The week here has brought us much closer. He rarely left your side, and then only if Rjoart guarded you in his place. That's not what's bothering me."

I'm about to ask when we turn the corner of a building to come upon the makeshift spaceport my fleet has taken residence on to find all of my soldiers and crew, but also not just the ten or so young adults I met earlier but more than a hundred Fernonians ready to leave, their belongings already on their shoulders and eagerly stepping from one foot to the other.

"It seems that when the boys went to get their stuff, more and more young men and women wanted to come and soon this happened. I'm not sure what you want me to do about it."

"Do all of them understand the conditions of working for me and that they might be in serious trouble someday?"

"They do and look forward to it. Heck, I'm not even sure they know they will be paid for the work."

"We can't take advantage of it, so have Hank work with Geraldine on a pay for them as cadets until their tests are finished. I almost wish I could place half of them with Ben's unit. They would scare the enemy away by their size."

"I'm sure Ben would agree with you. I'll try to have a look at their tests once they finish them and send the results of the most promising for his unit. We'll put a priority on the Army for those and see if they can go through the Army training afterward. If some fail, we can find them other work on the ships."

She leaves my side and joins Hank to talk about the tests and their goal for the young Fernonians. I just hope I don't run out of money before I start making money with my other plan. For that I need to get my other ships in one place and decide how to implement it.

After all the supplies, new recruits and regular personnel have left the surface of Fernon, it's time for my shuttle to leave. I wanted to be the last and make sure all goes well with the rest. Once in space it will be easier to solve problems. Just as the guard assembles next to the shuttle Hank walks up to me, his parents by his side. This can't be good.

"King, Queen, to what do I owe the honor of your visit just before we leave?"

"Although we do not agree with the prince's decision to be your bodyguard," the Queen says, "we would like to let you know that it has no bearing on how we appreciated your help in the battle. You risked your life and that of your fleet to defend a people you hardly know. Hank," she has difficulty getting out his name, "tells us that you never hesitated in committing your troops to battle. He tells us that there was nothing that could have changed your mind, that you never questioned who we were, but that someone was in danger and you had the means to help. We have a lot of history with your people, not all of it good, but you have changed many minds this past week. I hope to see more of you Admiral, and of your bodyguard I hope."

She ends with a smile as they leave. It must not have been easy for her to say her son's first name out in the open like that, and the memories inside tell me that she's right about the history of our people. Well, another good thing has happened out of that battle. Hopefully if more of us surface like I did they will continue in the same path as I.

We walk to the shuttle in silence and then make the trip to the *Red Widow* the same way. As the fleet prepares to head back to jump space and finally get to our next destination, a ship from the Peace delegation closes the gap with us and hails us. Captain Jackson is on the scene in front of me.

"Admiral Lebronski, Captain Ross and the rest of the Red Widow Group, I have heard that your destination is our home world of Peace. I wanted to let you know that you will be received like kings and queens on our world. Recordings of your battle here has already been sent to the Premier, and he agrees with me that you all have great courage and heart. Safe travels and I hope to see you there, if not to meet you again in battle, side by side from the start this time Captain Ross." She finishes with a quirky smile.

The fleet soon after speeds up to jump space and soon we

arrive at Peace, where we are as mentioned received as kings and queens. The Premier himself receives me and a few chosen ones while the rest take shifts to come down to the planet for some well-deserved R&R. The stay at Peace takes much longer than anticipated as the Premier has asked to update all of our sick bays in every ship and equip the larger ones with surgery equipment should the need arise.

He mentions that what we did at Fernon will go a long way to help their own relations with the system and wants to thank us for it. We also talk business opportunities as I lay out some of my beliefs that all races should be more intertwined for the Alliance to form a real entity and he agrees if all participate. That has always been the problem he explains as some take advantage of the others.

While in the Peace system I ask Geraldine to send a message to all ships I own to present themselves in a system that no race has claimed and seems empty of anything. They are given coordinates and should not leave until they have talked to the owner. I also have a personal request that involves a friend of hers back on Alexandria. It's time to kick my plans into high gear, now that they become clearer every day.

We say goodbye to our new friends, and I feel satisfied that the visit is a success. Not only are our ships better equipped to help my people in battle, or after the battle, but every member of the Group has had time to relax on a beautiful world with, I have to agree with Diana, the population being all great looking. It has to be that fresh air and huge forests all over the planet.

Our next destination is the same as all my other ships. This one will be tricky as the group that will already be at the location will far outnumber the fleet I have with me, so I need an edge. Time to call that great engineer Hector told me about, Augustine Henry.

She arrives at my quarters not sure why she's been called up. Hank lets her in and closes the hatch. Normally he would enter with the person, but I made him promise not to do that this time.

"Good morning Augustine, please take a seat."

"Thank you, Admiral."

"Please, call me Sherry. I've got enough Admiral from Commander Ionicci every day to last me a lifetime."

"Yes Admiral, I mean Sherry."

"I have a special project for you, and I need it on a very tight deadline. Hector told me you're the person for the job."

"I am Sherry, anything you need, the crazier the better."

"Good, cause this will sound crazy."

I lay out what I need and I see her eyes go big and her brain work overtime right in front of me. And to make matters worse for her, I need two things from her. Her deadline is a week, which will be the time it will take us to get close to the location I gave the other ships.

The rest of the trip is uneventful and almost boring compared to what's happened to us so far since I'm in charge, but I need to love this nothingness, because if my plans work out, in the end that is what life will be in the Alliance, boring and peaceful.

A few hours before arriving at our staging point, I take a walk into engineering to find my miracle worker, only to find that she has none of the items I asked her to make. Her office is pristine and she's just going through reports on the engine performance. I look at her and she signs for me to close the door. I do so and Hank makes sure no one bothers us.

"It took me some time to figure it out but I did."

"That's great Augustine, but I need them in a few hours and you don't seem to have any done." I say a little annoyed.

"Oh, they're not here. After what happened on our trip to Glengarry, I didn't want to take a chance that someone else could get wind of your plan and let the others know, so I stash them all in my quarters."

"How small are they? I know you're now head engineer on the ship, but your quarters can't be that big."

"They're actually very small but I rarely sleep in them. I spend almost all of my time in engineering. As for how big they are, about the size of a pad, and almost as thin. No one will be able to detect them. All you have to do is find a way to attach them to the right position on each ship without anyone noticing."

"Excellent. I've got the right person for the job. You'll have to tell them where to…"

"Sorry Admiral, but I have to do this myself. No one else knows exactly where to place them and if you find someone else, will you be able to trust them?"

"I don't like this. If you get caught, there's no knowing what they'll do to you."

"Oh, they won't catch me Sherry, hell they won't even see me."

Now I am curious. What has she got up her sleeve? She heads to a closet like space in her office and slowly takes out a suit, a spacesuit for that matter, but unlike any I've seen before. On its back are what seem like rockets and an extra-large air tank. But the material is almost black and none reflective. She sees me staring and is about to explain when Hank puts his head in the door.

"People coming, and I just got a message from Captain Ross that we are five minutes from normal space."

He ducks back out of the room and now I need to take a decision I don't want to take.

"Fine, I'll let you do it, but promise me you'll abort if anything feels out of place. I'll find you a ride over there."

I leave as she places her suit back in its hiding place. I enter the situation room after we've gotten back to normal space and a few messages from the captains are on my board, but I ignore them for now. I have more pressing matters to attend to. I dial a particular Captain's personal line, one that will go directly to his ear piece and not to the ship.

"Nathan, are you in a position to talk?"

By using his first name I let him know it's personal.

"I am Sherry, what's up?"

"I need you to take a few people and their cargo to the rest of the fleet. I also need you to take the pulse of the captains there and be ready to bail my engineer out of any situation she might find herself in."

"Well, this sounds interesting. Anything I need to know about?"

"Not on the air. I'll tell you personally when you come and pick her up."

"overcautious, when do you need me?"

"Now."

"On my way."

8

Chapter 8

The jump to the rest of the fleet is only a short distance and takes an hour in jump space. Upon re-entering normal space I'm nailed to my screens to see all of the action first hand. The next minutes might determine if my plans for a unified Alliance when the enemy comes will come true. And if that enemy's first volley was at Fernon, then we are in a rush to unify.

The coordinates I gave the fleet to assemble is a way off the jump point we'll be entering the system at, so it should give us a chance to judge the character of each Captain of all the ships that have showed up. From the data given to me by Geraldine, if all have showed up there should be almost two hundred ships waiting for us. I doubt all of them have made it but hopefully a lot of them did. Augustine's message had only said she was done, nothing else.

We enter normal space and my sensors light up with so much dots that it seems there is a sea of ships out there. All are waiting at the coordinates I gave them which is good, but something inside me doesn't like the closeness they have. If all of them have a devotion to my dead husband then I would have to replace almost two hundred crews, and that could take years, time I do not have.

Elena directs our ships toward them at a slow pace, as if we're some more of the ships coming for the reunion. Soon the comm blinks as a direct message comes in. Elena takes it for now.

"This is the *Widow*, what do you want?"

Elena purposefully does not mention the change in name so as not to tip our hand that we're the group they've been waiting for.

"This is Captain Devin North bitch, and you will show me the respect due me. Where the hell's the captain of your ship, I will deal with him alone."

I remember Devin North being mentioned a few times by Alan as his favorite of all his ship's Captains. Well, this should be fun.

"I am the captain of this ship asshole, and you will show me the courtesy of talking to me with the same respect as all the other Captains."

The venom in Elena's voice is genuine I can tell. She hates this bastard.

"Bullshit bitch, Alan would never put a woman as Captain."

"Well, this ain't Alan's fleet anymore prick, this is Admiral Sherry-Ann Lebronski's fleet, and you better not forget it."

So much for keeping it secret for long. Oh well, now that the cat's out of the bag, time to have fun. I take over the conversation.

"Captain North, you may have been my husband's favorite, but you are far from being mine. You will refrain from using foul language against women or you will be removed from

113

command, do I make myself clear?"

"You little bitch! If you think you can come here expecting us to kneel at your feet and surrender what you stole from the rightful owner you are seriously deluded."

"I warned you Captain North. It was nice knowing you."

I cut the connection and I open a channel to the *Trickster*.

"Nathan, pull the plug, will you?"

"With pleasure Admiral."

Several ships have started their engines and moved toward us but suddenly all of the ship engines, shields, weapons and basically everything except life support and comms is down on all ships except Nathan's. He moves his ship clearly in the view of all the others letting them know that he's responsible for their predicament and then moves off a bit to wait for us. Elena moves the fleet toward them and stops at a fair distance.

I open a channel to the whole fleet this time.

"By now all of the ships that did not try to hunt us and shoot us down can respond to Captain Ross directly and ask her where you can place your ship for now. Your engines will be placed back online but be warned that we are watching you closely. As for the others, you now find yourself with a Captain that has lost his head, literally. On your bridge you will find a Xirtan assassin that gladly works for me. They will take out any who resist and believe me when I say none of your ships have enough people in it to stop one of them. Just think of the time before we came into the system if you remember him or her being on the bridge? The answer is no but they have been there for hours already.

I already knew which ships to watch more closely because of the great work Captain Williams did in digging the worst Captains among you. My proposition to all ships is simple.

If you wish to have a life of adventure, great battles, life and death situations that will really matter in the history of the Alliance, then stay on the ship you are on and follow me. If you only want to disrespect people in general and rule them, you can step out of the ship, right now."

"But there is nothing out there, we'll die." Someone said.

"Exactly, because that option will be far better than if one of my people gets a hold of you. My friend Weil, one of my personal guards, loves people that disrespect me. Oh, did I forget to mention Weil is Brandari?"

I can almost hear the gulps from hundreds of men. This is fun.

"Think of one thing before you take your decision. If, in the little time that has pass since my husband died, I have been able to get people so dedicated to me to go alone aboard a ship and kill the captain right in front of all the rest of the crew, what could I do for you in the years to come? I take care of my people, personally and monetarily."

Now comes the big surprise that none of my crew knows about. I got a message from a friend not long after we left Peace and I asked for a little favor, one that might tip the scale in my favor. I let my ships know someone will be coming in system soon, so they are not too worried when ten ships suddenly appear on the radar at another jump point.

"One more thing, I have great friends." I finish to the whole fleet.

"Happy to see you again Admiral Lebronski. Are you having any trouble we might help you with?" Captain Jackson says to all the ships in the system. "You know how we hate people that hurt our friends."

Every person in the Alliance knows that if the citizens of

Peace name you friend, you will have their wrath if you so much as look at them funny. And although they are a peaceful people, they have a large fleet of excellent ships.

"No problem at all Captain Jackson, at least I don't think. Do I have a problem Captains?" I ask.

One after another the Captains of the ships already on route to the second location all give their loyalty to me, some faster than others. As for the ones that are still with their systems off, each of the Xirtan assassins gives the crews loyalty, if forced a bit. We will have to split those crew up.

"It seems I have no problem at all Hailey. Oh, and thanks for the incredible welcome we got from the Premier. I'm sure your advance notice helped him make that incredible dinner for us. The whole crew loved your world."

"My pleasure Sherry. Your saving Fernon did most of the work for you, I only mentioned how you saved the race from extinction."

With that she turns her ships around and leaves. Hailey had been the one to put together the little speech we just had. I do mean speech because none of that was for us but for the rest of the ships that had not been at both locations. Now all of them know that we're the ones that saved the Fernonians from disaster, which they probably have heard rumors about already, and they also know that we had a great relaxing time on Peace. If that can't solidify my hold on most of them then I don't know what will.

Elena comms me personally.

"Nice surprise boss, would have been nice to know about it."

"Sorry Elena, I never got a chance to be alone with you after Hailey suggested it, and I didn't want to say it in front of everyone. You know how fast rumors flow on a ship, and then the next day the whole fleet knows."

"Yep, I know, all of the captains in the fleet have congratulated me on my relationship with Hank. Heck I wasn't even sure we could call it a relationship since we see each other so little."

"Well, I'll have to remedy to that. I'll ask him to train a few of the new Fernonian recruits to take his place during some of your time off shift, and I won't take no for an answer Hank, I know you're listening."

"Hi sweetie, love you."

I look back at Hank and swear his rocky skin is a bit red. I smile at him and it definitely gets redder than before. I laugh a little and turn back to Elena.

"He's blushing, isn't he?" she asks.

"Yep, he is."

"Alright I'll leave you to prepare your next surprise, I have a ship to run. Some of us actually have a job you know."

She slams the comm shut before I can reply to her.

The next step I have is another job for Nathan, but this time with his group. I will have to find a name for them as I keep using them together and they work great that way. I don't want to use their smuggling background as a basis for their name, but something that will express how much of a pain they can be to the enemy. Oh, I've got it. I need to call him before I forget.

"Captain Williams, I would like to see you and the other Captains of the Rose's Thorn aboard as soon as you can free yourself."

"I'm sorry the what? Oh, you mean me and my three pains in the asses. Got it Admiral, we'll be right there."

About an hour later all four Captains enter a room up to

now unused on the *Red Widow*, or at least unused since I got the ship. I had a few crewmen turn it into a conference room so I can meet with various people, including dignitaries and Captains of my fleet. All four sit down while I'm going through some last-minute data Diana gave me earlier. Hank as usual is present for this meeting, he is always present. I've gotten used to the fact that I will rarely be alone anymore.

The four are as different from each other as any group could be. Nathan is thirty-four, average height and weight, good looking and a nice smile. Xavier Brookes is twenty-seven, six eight and almost two hundred and fifty pounds of pure muscle, has a large scar on his face and is far from the cutest man I've seen, but he has a genuine smile when he turns my way. Rebecca Burton is thirty-one, barely above five feet and I doubt she tips the scale at one twenty-five, but her golden locks go down to her butt and also has an incredible smile. The last of the four is Angie Lavender, a Railien of over six feet, thin as straw with a large head typical of the race. They are what old Earth thought of when they talked of aliens. Their level of intelligence is far greater than most races.

"So, Admiral, what's up?" Nathan asks.

Rebecca, sitting next to him, hits him in the arm and looks daggers at him.

"Nathan you idiot, show some respect. The Admiral will talk when she's good and ready. Sorry Admiral, he's always been an ass."

I smile at the banter between the two of them and the other two seem to be used to them bitching at each other. That is when I decide I can never separate these four crews, ever.

"It's OK Rebecca I've grown accustomed to the way Nathan talks and acts. In fact, let's cut the formalities and go on a first name basis, it will make this meeting go a lot faster."

"All good on our side Sherry. What can we do?"

I hand them each a pad with information no one else outside of me, Diana, Elena and Hank know about. This is the main reason I wanted to have the whole fleet here.

"On these pads you'll find information that is far beyond top secret, at least for now. Most of the information you will only get after completing a certain task."

"A wild goose chase, nice." Says Xavier.

"No bone head, it's to prevent us from having too much information at once and also to make sure that if something happens to us no one else can have the information on that pad." Replies Angie.

"Angie's right. I trust you four with my life, but what you will undertake is dangerous and that is why the secrecy installed on the pads. I wouldn't ask anyone else this. You four have not only the brains to pull it off, but the audacity it will take to make it to the end. This might take a long time, so on the pads are several accounts set up by Diana with enough funds to go the distance and more. You will need most of that money I'm sure and I will have her monitor the accounts to make sure you do not run dry. You also have on there a personal comm number to reach me directly at all times. If by any chance you meet with any of the fleet on your travels, try to stay away as much as possible. If for some reason I am unreachable, you also have numbers for Hank, Diana and Elena, Captain Ross." I add at their puzzled look about Elena's first name.

"Any questions?"

"A million, but none at the moment and I know most will answer themselves as we go. When do we leave?"

"As soon as possible."

"Well, I'm ready, how about you guys?" Nathan asks.

The other three nod and get up. Each salute me and Hank and then leave the conference room. Hank turns to me when the hatch closes.

"I do say this is your riskiest business yet. This could jeopardize everything you're trying to do."

"It could also cement it together. You know that Hank, you were at the meeting."

"I know, but why send those four? Their rogues, misfits. Hell, they were criminals before Captain Sillens brought them on."

"Yes, that is the exact reason I chose them. They have the knowledge to evade capture, to find what is impossible to find."

"You know that one day you will be wrong about something. I just hope it is not this."

"That makes two of us."

Now that the mission is given to what I believe to be the right person, I need to find a home for all of my ships and their crew. We cannot just keep flying all over the systems with no place to call home. The memories have given me just the place. I head for the situation room and comm Elena to give her the coordinates to the old Conranian planet.

"Are you sure about this Admiral? They say it is impossible to navigate and a death trap for anyone who goes there."

"I know Captain, but I need you to trust me on this. Please make sure that we enter normal space in front of everyone else and do not fire upon anything in the system."

"This comes from your memories you've been telling me about, isn't it?"

"It does."

"Good enough for me. I'll give the orders and set the course."

She cuts the comm and I sit back in my seat. The last month or so has been tiring in so many ways, but also satisfying like nothing I could ever have imagined. Back then my only concern was staying alive, now I have thousands of people counting on me making the right decisions to keep them safe. I lean back in my seat and fall asleep.

9

Chapter 9

I wake to sounds of explosions all over the ship, the alarms blaring and Hank trying to wake me up. What the hell's happening? Oh no, the Conra system. I fell asleep which means I have not communicated with the security system of the defense moons and now my fleet is being destroyed. How could I be so stupid?

The memories have told me of this, a large fleet would trigger the defense system and that none of today's ships would be able to live through a battle with the defense moons. I need to stop this and ask the ships to leave the system until I can disarm it.

"Elena, get every ship you can out of here before they're destroyed. I need to contact the defense system."

No response from the bridge.

"Elena?"

"Ma'am, the bridge is gone. We can barely control the ship as it is." Says one of the people at the consoles in front of me.

"What's the casualty rate?

"At least half the fleet is gone and the rest is not far behind."

"Get everyone out of here now!"

"We can't Admiral, none of our engines have enough power for it."

Oh my God, what have I done? I decided to come here and now my whole fleet will be destroyed and with it any hope of the Alliance in surviving the war to come.

"Enemy fire coming in. Evasive maneu..." the person never finishes as a flash of light so intense that it burns my eyes before going through my body.

I wake with a start, look around at the people working quietly on the consoles, Hank relaxing by the hatch. No explosions, no death, just a nightmare. Where are we now?

I look at the sensors and we are only ten minutes from the Conra system and suddenly the nightmare comes to the front of my mind. Not a nightmare, a premonition of what's to come. I slam my hand on the comm to all of the ships in my fleet.

"This is Admiral Lebronski, all stop right now!" I scream in the comm.

The people in the room are startled and look at me like I'm crazy. They might be right but I'm not going to take that chance.

I feel the ship coming out of jump space and see on the sensors that all have done so in a fairly tight formation. The comm flashes and I answer.

"Admiral, what's going on?" Elena says worried.

"It's a trap. I can't explain how, but I know it is."

"Your damn memories again?"

"I believe so yes."

"They haven't been wrong yet. What do you want to do now?"

"I'm not sure. Get a conference ready between all Captains.

Place Captain Waxman on the main screen. I want you and the guard there in ten."

"On my way."

I get up and follow Hank out to the conference room. By the time I get there all the captains are connected and Kevin is on the main screen, the guard is all there and Elena comes in a second behind me.

"Alright Admiral, you've got us on line, what's going on?" Elena asks.

"For those Captains that do not know, I'm Conranian and several weeks ago memories have started coming back to me on my people and my abilities. Just before I called out a full stop, I had a vision of us entering the destination system and being completely whipped out. Exactly what destroyed us is still unclear, but I remember thinking of Defense Moons and communicating with the defense system to shut it off.

The first thing I need to figure out is how to communicate with the system without any of you being in harm's way. The second will depend on the first."

"Do you think it's possible this might just be a regular nightmare?" one of the other Captains asks.

"Coming here I thought of it, but then I remembered my first day. The first time my power surfaced I had a dream very similar to this one, of being attacked by Vuldalians, and upon awakening, I found my life threatened by two large men that were later identified as Vuldalians agents. The chance of this one being just a simple nightmare are too low for me to risk any of your lives."

"What are you saying?" asks Brad

"I'll need to go there alone before the fleet joins me."

The loud yelling that ensues almost blows me off my chair,

and not just from the conference room people. The static on the line with the other Captains makes Kevin's face freeze up once in a while, so I cannot catch anyone's words properly. I lift my hands for silence then realize that most of them cannot see me.

"Please Captains, let me explain."

The noise level takes a few seconds and then goes deadly quiet.

"The defense moons around the whole system are designed to destroy anything larger than a shuttle and seriously armed when it enters the space. An armada of over two hundred ships will have them flooding the space with missiles, ship blasters and other weaponry that none of us have ever seen. Although my people have been gone for close to a thousand years, their technology is still more advanced than ours. We just cannot beat it. I need to go alone."

"And just how will you get there? Can you pilot a jump capable shuttle?" Kevin asked.

I know where he's getting at and that is the part, I hate the most.

"No, I cannot."

Another argument starts but I cut this one short.

"I will need a pilot for the shuttle. This person will have to volunteer him or herself, not the captain that volunteers that person. Also, it cannot be any of the captains, or the guard, or you Hank. The volunteer will be selected among the few who place their names forward. I ask you the captains to share this with your crew and let them decide for themselves. I want no pressure from anyone."

An hour later I ask the captains to submit the names of the people that have volunteered for the piloting job. When I get the list with thousands of names on it, I know I have to reduce that number considerably. I remind the captains that this might very well be a one-way trip for the pilot as I do not know how I will be able to protect that person. I give them another hour to confer with their crew and the list comes back with a few more names. It seems that basically anyone who can pilot a shuttle has volunteered, even the captains, the guard and Hank. So much for my guidelines.

It brings a tear to my eye that I might be choosing someone for slaughter, and that almost every single person that qualifies to fly a shuttle, and probably a few that don't, have still placed there name in knowing the danger just to make sure I got there safe and the rest of the fleet might also be safe.

I ask Diana to lend me her computer, enter the information in it, and then start filtering. With time slipping away, I need to make a decision quickly, so her Kroh tech will come in handy at this moment. I take out all the people I said could not go, all that do not qualify for jump space shuttles or have less than five years experience, and a few other qualifiers and come up with a list of over a hundred names still. Next, I ask the computer to take out the names of people with young kids. The parents need to be around for them to grow correctly, so I will not chance one of them on a mission I am almost sure will end with that person's death. This leaves me with a dozen names.

I don't want to be the one to make the choice, so I ask the computer to choose the perfect person for a mission such as this based on the information it has on each person. It comes up with one name: Chicago. Why would someone name their kid after a city on Earth? No last name or much information on him. Early forties, excellent fighter pilot, twenty years of experience, reserved and always there when you need him. I can't find anything to refuse this result, so I make the call to Captain Jerry McNiven of the *Sunshade*, a fighter support ship that joined us from the rest of the fleet. McNiven did not lose his head in the last system, so I have no reason to doubt his loyalty or that of his fighter pilot.

"Captain McNiven, this is Admiral Lebronski. Would you have Chicago transfer over to my ship please so he can accompany me?"

"Chicago ma'am, really? Damn, he's the best damn fighter pilot I've ever seen, but if anyone can make sure you survive that little trip of yours than he's your man. What ship will you be taking Admiral?"

"I'm not sure yet Captain, why?"

"Chicago's fighter is a modified light freighter. It has jump capability and has more weapons than some small warships. And more importantly it has a place for a passenger. I would suggest he joins you in his ship ma'am, if that is acceptable for you?"

"I'd hate to take away not only your best pilot but also a great ship."

"No one else can even come close to piloting that beast ma'am. Chicago's got a gift, and that might mean the difference between you and maybe even him surviving the outcome of your trip."

"Then I accept your offer Captain McNiven. Thank you."

"My pleasure Admiral. I have to say I never liked your husband, but with a wife, two exes and ten kids to take care of, he paid the bills."

"Why don't the exes cover some of the cost of those kids?"

"I asked them not to. I want them to concentrate on making

sure the kids don't run off into the bad side of the law and become great citizens instead of people like your husband was. It's OK Admiral, I like flying more than I like my wives. I tend to have very poor taste in women and find myself flirting with the worse kind. Not the best of traits I know, but I just love women too much. Sorry Admiral for expanding so much into my personal life."

"That's OK Captain, I like knowing more about my employees. Do you treat your wife and exes with respect Captain?"

"Why do you think I have three of them? Even if they've had enough of me not being there for them, they still hang around all the time. So much so that my exes and my current wife are always together. I guess I'm doomed the next time I head home. They probably have a plan to make me pay dearly my long absence. I'll send Chicago right away Admiral."

A few minutes later a craft leaves *Sunshades*'s bay and makes its way to ours. I turn my screens over to the external cameras to watch this intriguing fighter that Jerry talked about. It's soon obvious this is not a standard fighter as he had mentioned, and the turned freighter makes me think of smugglers trying to get drugs into a system. Since the craft is small it doesn't leave much of a footprint on the space around it and seems far more maneuverable than any larger freighter. The perfect combination for what I have in mind, if we both survive this next trip.

I get up as the craft enters our bay and Hank leans away from the wall and follows. He probably wants to get a last go at me before he has to let me go alone with Chicago. It won't work anyway but he might still try. The elevator ride is silent as is the rest of the walk to the bay, so my hopes are up that I can simply go about my trip without another argument. Hank had not been silent during the waiting periods as the names were accumulated. He did not mind dying if it meant I would survive he had said.

That hope is crushed as the hatch to the bay opens. The large fighter or small freighter sits on the ground with the side hatch open and Chicago I'm guessing leaning against the side of the craft. But the problem is the whole guard waiting for me between the bay hatch and the craft. I'm not sure what their planning but all of them are armed to the teeth.

'They don't plan on letting you go alone.' Diana says in my mind.

'Did you try and persuade them?'

'I don't plan on letting you go alone.'

'And if I order you to stand down?'

'We plan on being depth for the next few minutes.'

Suddenly Chicago leans away from the craft and places himself in what I've grown to understand is a fighting stance.

"As I understand it Admiral, you plan on coming with me alone on this trip, am I right?" Chicago's deep voice sounds from the other side of the guard.

In a rush of speed Rjoart liberates his sword and heads for my pilot, probably intending on making sure he doesn't make the trip. But something incredible happens, the blade meets another blade, one that starts to glow with a blueish light. Chicago grins as if he finally meets a foe worth fighting and all hell breaks loose in the bay.

The rest of the guard follows a surprised Rjoart and pull out their weapons but try as they might, none of them can get a hit in on Chicago. I've never seen anyone move that fast, and I have the best fighters in the Alliance in my guard. This goes on for only a minute but it seems to last an hour. What stops the battle for a few second is the first wound Rjoart has ever gotten from a foe, a sword cut on his sword arm. The cut barely bleeds, in fact it mostly becomes reddish, but it's enough to stop the guard and stare at the man they've been trying to kill and failing.

"Enough!" I yell in the sudden silence.

No one turns toward me except Chicago, a glint in his eyes like he's enjoying himself immensely. I walk to the group and look directly into his eyes. He straightens and salutes me. I stare into his eyes without acknowledging his salute.

"You enjoy fighting Chicago?"

"I enjoy fighting warriors deserving of the name when I do not have to kill them. I know who these are and how important they are to the fleet and you. I would never hurt one of them."

"A few minutes ago I would have called that bravado, but after what I've seen I think you might just deserve to say this. Where did you learn to fight like that?"

"On my home world of Hell Admiral. There I grew up in a foster home with twenty other children that were older and larger. I was the only one that got off the planet between them. The others got into the gangs and died soon after."

"I'm sorry for your loss."

"I'm not Admiral, they were all pricks. I got off the world and found a job with a freighter as a deck hand, and soon we were attacked by pirates. When they boarded the freighter, none got back off. I could not let them kill my new family. The fleet is my family now Admiral and my pledge is the same as it was then."

Rjoart puts his sword away and the others follow suit. Then one after the other they salute him in their own little way, Aaron giving him the finger with Chicago replying with a wink, and then the guard leaves the bay satisfied that I will be safe with my new pilot. Hank is beside me at that point and he's staring daggers at Chicago. The pilot bows to him and extends his hand for Hank to shake. Hank mirrors the gesture and then leaves the bay as well.

I turn to Chicago with a questioning look.

"In Fernonian culture, when someone bows to them and then extends their hand, it means that person is taking responsibility for the charge the other has, in this case you. By doing the same to me, he agrees to give me responsibility. Now I really don't have a choice in bringing you back safely Admiral, because although I can hold your warriors off, barely I have to add now, I would have no chance against a full grown Fernonian in a fury."

"I believe you there. I saw him go through dozens of enemies when he needed to get to the Palace on Fernon."

"Shall we Admiral?"

I nod and walk inside his fighter. The hatch leads to a cramped corridor that leads to engineering on one side and the cockpit on the other. I head for the cockpit and find it almost sparkling clean. Not sure why this surprises me but it does. My small hesitation pulls a comment from him.

"Expecting a mess?"

"I was frankly, I'm sorry for thinking poorly of you."

"Don't be Admiral. Most fighter pilots keep their rooms a mess but will always have their cockpits spotless. Anything not bolted down is a potential threat in a dogfight so we make sure that this stays as clean as a sanctuary."

"And is your room clean Chicago?" I ask a bit teasingly.

"You can go have a look if you want Admiral. I always sleep in engineering. I live a simple life."

"That's OK, I believe you. Do you live like this because my husband was not paying you enough?"

"No, I got compensation enough, but I live to fly so as long as I have enough credits to feed myself, I'm good."

I sit in the brand-new seat while he takes the perfectly used one on the left. I buckle in as I'm sure it will be a very bumpy ride while Chicago starts the pre-flight sequence and then buckles up as well. Soon we have the green light to exit the bay as everyone has left and he slowly takes it out the bay and into space. Although I've seen space on the many screens on the *Red Widow*, I've never been so close to being in space as the view in front of us is not from a screen but from a window. I must have a stunned face because he asks.

"First time seeing it live Admiral?"

"Yes, it is, and please call me Sherry. Before inheriting from my husband, I'd never left Alexandria, so all of this is new to me. I'm learning as I go."

"Well, you're doing a hell of a good job so far Sherry, so just keep doing what you've been doing and all will go to your liking."

"I hope you're right Chicago, I really do."

"Ready to face death Sherry?"

"As ready as I'll ever be. Hit it."

And he does, more so than I thought possible. One second, we're flying slowly next to my ship and the next we're hitting jump space. The timer on the console indicates that we'll hit regular space in less than eight minutes, which is two minutes less than the fleet would have taken. Fast ship.

"So, Sherry, what are we expected to face on the other side?"

"From what I've seen in the premonition and what the memories remember, there should be at least a dozen security moons armed better than the largest warship we have now, thousands of space mines, and sentry ships that are fast and agile."

"A breeze then. Anything deadly in that mix?" he asks with a wink.

"If you're as good at flying as you are at fighting, we might actually survive long enough to get to the planet and deactivate the system."

Chicago nods and turns to his controls. At a minute before coming out of jump space he starts a flurry of button punching and nob turning, not stopping until we're about five seconds from regular space. We come out of jump space and into the system known as Conra, where the seat of my ancestors was before it was destroyed by the Vuldalians. I reach out with my senses trying to find the moons and other security objects but find none close by. I look at Chicago and he smiles.

"A little trick I learned in my freighter days. Good systems are able to detect someone coming to their space a good five minutes before they appear, so my teacher showed me a trick when you have a good enough ship where you wait for the last minutes and then start switching jump points constantly, therefor confusing the operator at the other end, either a pirate as on the occasion he showed me, or in this case the system controlling the defense of Conra. The jump point we came out of is on the other side of the system, so we might have a few seconds more to reach the planet before they reposition and attack us."

I'm not sure I understand everything he told me but I know that none of the moons are close enough to shoot at us yet. Halfway to the planet five ships appear on the long-range sensors and Chicago becomes silent once more in concentration. I again reach my senses out and find the ships there waiting for me, but they won't obey my commands.

"I can't seem to get control of them."

"That's OK Admiral, just do what you can and I'll do the rest."

The ship soon comes in range of their weapons and they waste no time waiting to get a better shot. Although I can't get control, I can still feel them and tell where they are shooting.

"Turn right." I say almost too late and Chicago turns the ship, one of the blasters hitting the edge of our shields.

Knowing what to look for I can now feel a bit quicker where they fire and the next couple of volleys, I can advise Chicago sooner and he easily evades the blasters and soon the missiles add another dimension. Something strange happens the next volley as Chicago turns just before I advise him. The next volley I feel I do not have to say anything, risking our lives on a hunch, and the pilot turns the ship as if I was not there. He can feel them also. That can only mean one thing: Chicago is Conranian.

"I can't evade them Admiral and shoot at them. Mind doing the honors?" he points at the controls in front of me.

I've never piloted a ship before or fired weapons, but some of the memories I have help me figure out most of it and soon I start shooting blasters at the five ships, not hitting anything. The sensors start screaming at us and I look to find two defense moons gaining speed. This is a losing battle if I can't gain control of the defense system. I concentrate on the ships closest to us and try to evaluate where they will be when my blasters hit them, and fire at one of them hitting the edge of its shields.

"Feel them the same way as you did, but this time concentrate on their movement instead of their aim." Chicago says.

I do just that and the next target does exactly as I felt so I poor everything we have at it and the shields go down and the haul gets some damage. This will take forever at this rate, so I turn to my pilot and tell him to gun it for the planet. I can see it now; it's charred remains pitiful compared to what it once must have been. Four moons have set up a defensive position in front of us and there is no way Chicago will be able to penetrate their position so he turns left and tries to go around them only to find the other moons either move to block us or other moons are waiting for us around the planet.

Time for desperate actions, so I use the power inside me to reach out to the planet looking for the system. After a couple seconds that feel like hours, I detect something, a source of power that is sending a signal all over the system. This has to be it, but it will not respond to my touch. I can't believe I came all the way to the home world of my people only to die at the hands of a defense system centuries old. As I did back on Fernon, I dig deep inside the pool of power radiating inside me and draw on all of it to gain access to the system and stop it.

The searing pain is nothing compared to what losing my entire fleet would be so I push on, drawing more and more power. I cannot even feel the pain anymore as none of my nerves survive the surge in power and even Chicago next to me has to protect his eyes as an intense beam of light passes right through the ship in the direction of the planet and that station sending information to the rest of the defense system. Suddenly the ships and moons stop their attack on our little ship but I'm unable to stop the climbing power inside me. It needs release and I'm afraid that it will consume me if I let it out.

Then Chicago does what I said no one in my fleet can ever do, he hit's me right across the jaw and darkness takes me once again.

10

Chapter 10

Soft light greets me as I open my eyes in my room, the soft sheets under me feel great after the enormous pain I felt last time I was conscious. The left side of my jaw feels raw and I can feel a bandage there, no doubt from the blow I took from my pilot, who probably saved my life in the most unusual way.

Next to me sits Hank, the usual large presence very comforting at the moment but the fact that the rest of the guard is also there less so. Where is Chicago? Hank would not need the guard here unless something bad has happened. I turn to my bodyguard and softly ask.

"Where is Chicago?"

"The traitor is in the brig, awaiting execution."

"What?" fully awake now. "Get him out of there now and bring him to me."

"But Admiral, he tried to kill you." Hank says.

"None sense, now please do as I say."

Hank nods to Brad who personally leaves the room with Rjoart to bring my pilot. The ten minutes it takes them to get him I try to remember anything about the flight to the Conra system. Finally, the three men arrive and I ask the guard to leave us, but none of them listen.

"Chicago, how are you doing?"

"Good Admiral."

"Hank, what the hell is going on here?"

Hank goes on to explain how after I was unconscious Chicago called the fleet over because he said it was now safe, but the defense system attacked them as soon as they came into the system. It took over two minutes for the system to shut down again, he does not know how. It seems that when I fell unconscious the system determined that I was in trouble and turned itself back on. Hank goes on to say that Chicago says he is the one that turned it off again.

"Guys, let Chicago go please. He only hit me to save my life, as the power was killing me. And I'm sure he did turn it off again because he's also Conranian."

The look of shock on all the people around me confirms my belief that none of them had thought of that possibility, all that is except Rjoart. I ask the assassin over so he can explain how he knew.

"I did not Admiral, but I had my doubts. No other could have survived a fight against all of us, wherever he was raised."

I nod and he follows the others out. I motion for Chicago to come closer and he does, giving Hank guarded looks.

"How long have you known you were Conranian?" I ask him.

"About a minute Admiral. My reflexes were always far above any other person and my senses warned me when danger was close, which explains my skill in battle as well as in a dog fight. Probably why I also keep to myself."

"Well, that will be hard to do now as everyone in the fleet

will know who you really are."

"Can't we keep it a secret Admiral?"

"By now the whole fleet knows you bested most of my guard single-handedly, and they are a little embarrassed by it I am sure, so they probably jumped at the notion that you're like me to explain how you were able to beat them. By the time you reach your ship to continue your work you will be a celebrity I'm afraid."

He looks more scared of that than of facing Hank. Strange man. He nods to me and Hank and then makes his way out the hatch. Now time to finish what I started. I grab my comm and call Elena.

"Good to hear you're up Admiral, what can I do for you?"

"Assemble all Captains to the *Hand of God*, they have the largest conference room. I want all of them there within two hours, no exceptions."

"Will do Admiral." And the connection cuts off.

"Commander, get the guard ready to join us and ask Major Stock to also join the meeting."

"It's actually Lieutenant-Colonel now Admiral. With all the Fernonians that came aboard, most wanted to join his group and all but a few that asked were able to pass the tests with flying colors as you would say."

"Well then ask him to meet us in person in the bay so I can congratulate him on the promotion. I can't wait to see the look on the faces of the next enemy that we encounter. My guess is that they drop their weapons as soon as they see all the Fernonians get off the transports."

With a smile I get up and after dressing into proper closes in my rooms I follow Hank to the bay where the guard is waiting. Chicago has already left the bay with his ship and preparations are being made to two attack shuttles. I stop the technicians right away and point to a pair of regular shuttles in the corner.

"We have no need for attack shuttles when going to one of our ships gentlemen. Please just make sure these are ready to go and then go get yourselves a good meal."

The guard as well as Hank look at me funny probably wondering why I have the bay cleared before I need to. The technicians finish checking the dual shuttles and head off for the meal. As they head out the hatch a hooded figure steps into the bay and heads straight for us. I feel the guard tense and reach for weapons, all but Diana who's probably reading the woman's mind at the present and knows she's not a threat. The hood is pulled back and the most stunning woman I've ever seen continues her way to us. By then most of the male guard members have completely forgotten about their weapons, but Diana brings them back to life.

"Good thing she's not pulling out a blaster cause you sorry bunch would be dead before you knew it." She walks to the new arrival. "My name is Diana Gnalls, and you are?"

"Katherine Lepage. Nice to meet you, Diana."

Now I understand why Geraldine used her to get my ex-husband to look the other way while he was signing the papers to hand over everything, he had to me. I find myself attracted to her and I love men, not women. The men rush to introduce themselves and I usher everyone in the shuttles. All want to be in the same one as Katherine, to learn more about her they say, but I have more important work than having the men screw up her cover by ogling over her.

So, as we head over to the meeting I share the shuttle with Diana, Katherine, Julie who's piloting at the moment, and Hank, the only man here, but his relationship with Elena and the fierce loyal trait of his kind do not make him a threat to the likes of Katherine. As soon as we clear the ship, I ask Julie to shut all comms coming in or going out.

"How did it go Katherine?" I ask.

Hank looks at me wondering what I'm talking about but Diana already knows since she probably read the full report inside her head.

"All went according to plan Sherry. Alvaro has settled fully into the role of business owner and the regular operations are increasing to a higher rate than expected. My guess as the cause of this rate is the way he treats the workers."

With a little anger in my voice, I ask her to explain.

"He's installed insurance for all employees, sick days and paid leave for emergencies, doubled the vacation days each employee has, hired a food company to deliver fresh food to the cafeteria on each operation to make sure the workers are well fed. Has cut overtime and hired more employees to compensate for the missing hours. The older and best of his employees he gave them promotions to lead the newer employees and show them the ropes.

The research section of the company has been running for a while now. He bought a new building for them so they would not be bothered by anything else and the people you hired got there just as the facility was finished. They are extremely efficient as they already finished ten of the suits by the time Angela sent in the electronics for them. In fact, she sent enough for a hundred suits on the first shipment and has promised a full thousand by the end of the month which should be in a few days. I'm not sure how you were able to pull it off but you might just have what you want out of both these deals."

Ignoring the stunned look on Hank's face, I continue with

Katherine.

"Were you noticed while gathering the info?"

"Alvaro was actually easy to spy on as most of his operation is an open book. For him employees should know how good the company is doing if they are to have a part in its success. The research part was a different matter but I was able to sneak in and gather the info. Just before leaving I left an info disk on his desk explaining how he needs to improve security there and the means to do it. I only signed that I was your agent."

"How are the company profits doing with all his expenses?"

"That's the funny part. With everything he's spent on extra personnel, extra equipment and the little luxuries he's now giving his employees, profits are up ten percent in the first full month of production after all these have been implemented."

"It's actually not surprising at all. Happy employees will give you way more of themselves if they feel the high command of the company cares for them. Good, now for your next assignment. I want you to walk around the *Hand of God* and take the pulse of the soldiers on it. I want to make sure they accept the new recruits and that none are resentful that their commander has taken them away from the ground and into space."

"Will do boss. The suits are in room forty-three 'C', all secure in their cases and ready for normal sized people, sorry Hank."

Hank doesn't even acknowledge her statement as he's still trying to figure out who this person is.

"Hank, she's the Secret Widow leader, our secret service people that I had created shortly after we left Alexandria. As of now we have five agents under Katherine in different places in the Alliance getting information for us that could help us cement this fragile Alliance."

"Six." Katherine says.

"What?" I ask.

"I have six people under my wing. I recruited that super cute pilot that left just before you got into the bay. Weird name though."

"Chicago's Conranian, so he'll be a great asset for you but a large loss for us. Captain McNiven won't be happy."

"Actually, he doesn't mind too much since you sent him on an important mission that might take months to complete."

"I never did anything like that."

"Sure, you did, just after he left the bay, he got a message from his Captain to report to the *Hand of God* and await a passenger. I did say he's cute."

"Do you think it prudent to let one with so much talent leave the fleet and go off on scouting missions?" Hank asks. "With him being the only other Conranian in your fleet, he can be very useful if something were to happen to you."

"I was not aware of him leaving before a minute ago, but now that I think about it, I like the idea of this man, obviously loyal, going around the systems and doing the dirty work the SW will need done. His skills in a fight will keep him alive where most would crumble under the numbers. If he can take on the full guard, there is nothing out there that will put him down."

"I find it fascinating how you adjust to any situation so quickly Admiral. I will say no more about this subject."

"Actually Commander, I would prefer if you did not say anything about anything that has been discussed in the shuttle. That goes for you also Julie and Diana. I cannot let anyone know about the SW as the Alliance frowns on corporations having their own secret agency. Now Diana, as soon as we land in the bay, I want you to book a meeting room, smaller this time, and send a message to all the guard where it is. I need to let you guys know what the plan is for the near future before telling the other Captains."

"Almost at the bay force field Admiral." Julie says from the pilot seat.

"Excellent Julie, thanks. Alright people, time to change the Alliance for the better."

The second we land Katherine is off to find her new bodyguard and Diana is off to find a meeting room. Half an hour before the big meeting I sit at the end of a large table with the rest of the guard. Also at the table are two newcomers that I trust with my life but some in the guard do not know them. I need to do something I have been dreading since the guard first formed, but it will be essential for the survival of the Red Widow Group and therefor the Alliance.

"First off I'd like to welcome to the guard two newcomers that I know will do their duty the same as all of you have in the past. They are both very capable security officers and will not hesitate to do anything to protect the Red Widow Group and its ships. First is from the *Promise*. Brenda Vixon has served on that ship for many years and when that idiot Anderson would sentence a crew for death, she always did her best to get them off the ship safely if they deserved a better treatment. Second is our very own Stephanie Blanche. Security for only a little bit of time, she has shown excellent skills in the Fernon battle, taking over the position of a fallen comrade and will definitely lighten the mood on any ship she serves on with her talent at being clumsy. Alright guys I'll cut to the chance right away. The reason I wanted to see you before the rest is that for the first time, I need to split you guys up. Some will argue but this is none negotiable. We have over two-hundred ships in the fleet at the moment, and I can't keep them all here. I need the fleet to protect our assets as well as our friends. But most importantly I need them out there to be visible and help out where they are needed.

The Alliance Navy is a joke with their fifty ships older than the Alliance itself, and all they protect are their bases. Several members have their fleets, but most have only their own concerns to think about. Then there's the large fleets of the corporations, like ours was, and those are the main problem. A lot of them are run by power hungry leaders that will stop at nothing to get richer. Those are the ones we will need to stop before the enemy makes his move.

Now, we have over two-hundred ships as I said, so I would like to form eight fleets of twenty-five ships each, all mixed with smaller and larger ships, and I will need one of you on the main ship of each fleet as my eyes and ears. The captain in charge will be leading the whole fleet he has, but I need you to make sure they follow our guidelines and the mission. Rjoart I would like you to ask your group if they would mind working for the rest of the guard? They would be a couple of them to each fleet so that if one of you has a problem you can have a solution at the ready."

We go on to separate the fleets and their locations. Soon the time for the meeting arrives and we head over to it. I'm glad to see that all of the captains are there as well as Ben Stock with a few of his command group. As there are no rooms equipped with enough tables and chairs to fit everyone, I asked Captain Voisin to simply clear the whole room and leave only a simple raised section so I can be heard and seen by every other Captain. I am surprised and glad to see that there is no order to the groups talking together, everyone talking to everyone else.

The room comes quiet as we enter and I make my way to the raised section followed closely by the guard who spread out close by but not too close to suggest they do not trust the captains. I go on to explain the plan to them as I did to the guard, leaving out only the part about Rjoart's crew and no objections arise from the group of men and women.

"We made the list of which ship goes on which fleet and who leads it." I send everyone the list on their comm units. "On there as well is the member of the guard coming with you and your assigned territory. Now as for Lieutenant-Colonel Stock's men, there are still too few of them to place even a squad on each ship, but we are working on correcting that situation. Are there any questions?"

A Captain I haven't met yet raises his hand.

"Yes sir, what is it? I'm sorry I do not know your name yet."

"Captain Hector Trenton Admiral, my ship is the *Flying Castle*. I'd like to know about the ships not on your fleet list? I do not see my ship on there."

"Excellent question Captain Trenton. The simple answer is you're mine." I smile as a few Captains laugh at that. "Seriously, all ships not on the list have a home port of this very system. Once every ship is on route to the destination system, we will head out to the fifth planet of this system and see what can be salvaged from the old Conranian Empire. If my calculations are correct, we will have twelve ships in system. That combined with the defense moons and the drone ships, once they are repaired, will make for a formidable defense. We can revise this situation as we get more ships."

Captain Paul Voisin raises his hand after.

"Yes Captain Voisin?"

"Admiral, you say that the navy's controlled by the major corporations are the problem. I agree, but I have a Captain friend in one of those fleets and she tells me that a lot of the crews and Captains do not agree with their leader's thinking. Maybe we could use this information to 'steal' some of the crews and their ships from the corps that treat them badly. We could call it a humanitarian mission."

After a good laugh the room quiets down again.

"Make me a list for now of the ones you know about as well as contact info for your Captain friend. I am totally for your 'humanitarian mission', but we need to make sure we don't put the Alliance on our bad side. They may not do a great job these days, but they are the Government in power and most of their laws make sense. We'll start this phase of our deployment and see where we stand in a few weeks or months."

No one else has any questions so the large group spreads out and forms smaller groups that will form the fleets we assigned. I leave them to it so that they may acquaint themselves with some Captains they do not know and with the member of the guard coming along. I give Stephanie a once over to make sure this isn't too much responsibility for such a young officer, but she walks over to her group with confidence and even takes the lead in presenting herself to the others.

Hank and I walk to where our twelve Captains have gone to meet and find there my own Captain Elena, Captain Voisin of the *Hand of God*, Captain Trenton of the *Flying Castle*, and the other nine in my group. I spend the next hour learning a little about each.

Melinda Jones is Captain of the missile boat *Challenging Arrow*, Henry Burns is Captain of the *Supernova*, a ship

147

equipped with an insane amount of heavy blasters, Forest Daniels is Captain of the *Ray of Light*, a support ship for in close fighting, Brent Deveraux is Captain of the *Silver Knight* which has a company of fighters in its belly, Jessica Chang Captains the *Dark Samurai*, a smaller ship with great armor and tons of medium blasters to go after fighter support before they hit the other ships, Benny Harrow Captains the *Shadow Ghost*, a long range support ship equipped with several Gauss rifles, Dan Levingston is Captain of the *Caracal*, a very fast and agile ship so it can go from one target to the other giving damage and getting away after, Madison Brooks is Captain to the *Longbow*, a sister ship of the *Shadow Ghost* and finally Helen Greaves, Captain to the oldest ship in my fleet but also the most dangerous one, the *Angry Grandpa*.

Most of these ships could have easily been part of any fleet we have, but the *Angry Grandpa* is far too slow to be of any use in any traveling fleet. As guard duty in the core system of our new little group, it is perfectly suited and I'm glad we have it. It far surpasses any other ship in the fleet in both armor and weaponry.

Once everyone has had a chance to chat and know each other a little bit I ask that they get on their way to their designated territory and my group heads to our own ships. When I arrive at our shuttle, I find the suits have been transferred to it which leaves little room for us but is well worth it. As soon as we arrive aboard the *Red Widow,* I ask Augustine to come and join me in the bay. I barely have time to say hello when she completely forgets I exist and goes straight for the nearest suit. I'm pleased at first when a lot of approving grunting comes out of her but then the critique grunts come and continue for many minutes. I clear my throat to get her attention.

"Oh my God Admiral I'm so sorry."

"That's OK Augustine. What do you think of them?" I ask waiting for the negative revue.

"Their awesome! A little tweak here and there will make them perfect for my crews that have to go out in space for repairs without fearing getting hit by space dust. The hidden weapon bays are perfect so they don't get in the way and if the techs find trouble coming while they work, they can dispatch it themselves instead of having to wait for the marines. The servos in the arms and legs help both the techs and the marines as they can carry larger and heavier equipment or weapons."

"Well, while you take a breath of air, I'd like to give you two of them to have fun with. I want one set up perfectly for techs in space and another for my marines both in space and in atmosphere. And please make blueprints of what you're making so I can send them to the factory. As they are now, they are perfect for planet side battles, but I would like some for future full-time marines aboard each ship."

"On it right away Admiral."

"You're not on anything at the moment?" surprise in my voice.

"I'm always working on something Admiral, but these suits are way more important. Oh, do you want me to make some for Fernonians as well?"

I turn to Hank next to me as always.

"Our hard skin protects us from most damage." Hank says.

"I know that my over-qualified bodyguard, but we saw on Fernon that even your superior skin and strength did not prevent some of you from dying. I'd like to give you the extra advantage so that none of you die. Also, as far as I know, you can't breathe in space."

149

"No, we cannot. If you require my presence Head Technician for the fitting I will comply."

"Is he always so formal Admiral?"

"Yep, he is."

Hank follows Augustine to engineering carrying two of the suits in his arms while Augustine pulls the other one on a cart. By the time I get to the intersection to the lifts Rebecca Ionicci, Hank's niece, shows up behind me and takes over guard duty while her uncle if off playing supermodel. It took her a full ten seconds to get in position as my protector which means Hank contacted her the second he knew he would be parading. Or he sent her a message inbound so she would be ready in case something came up. I wonder if she will tell me which it is? I turn to ask and see her smile.

"Why are you smiling Rebecca?"

"Because I just won the bet with my uncle, I mean Commander Ionicci."

"We're alone so you can be familiar. Which bet would that be?"

"That you would turn around within the first minute or after. I chose before one minute. You turned around at fifty-four seconds."

"And may I ask what the prize is?" I ask amused by this new personality of my chief guard.

"A basket of strawberries."

I raise my eyebrows at that.

"I wasn't aware your people eat strawberries. They are a fruit from old Earth that thankfully someone brought seeds to populate most worlds with them. Are there any on Fernon?"

"No. My first taste came a week ago when he showed me his secret stash of them in his room. My uncle rarely indulges in luxuries, but he told me that strawberries are his only vise."

"Apparently he also has gabbling to add to it. I hope you enjoy those strawberries Rebecca, you've earned them."

Oh Hank, you have not heard the last of this one. He just gave me, without his knowledge, some munition to bug the hell out of him for at least a few days.

I head for the bridge and find the second shift in command so I walk toward Elena's office adjacent to the bridge and the system captures my presence and is probably telling the captain that I'm waiting. Barely two seconds after stopping in front of the hatch it opens for me and I walk in to find Elena pouring herself a drink. She nods to the drink in a silent question if I want one but I refuse. I might take a nightcap before going to bed but that is still far away.

"Did you know that your love has an affinity for strawberries?" I say to open the conversation.

"What? He never told me that. How'd you find out?"

"He made a bet with his niece and the prize is a basket of strawberries."

"Where the hell will he find strawberries in this part of space?"

"In his room fridge."

"That cheating bastard, no wonder he always offered to get me a drink when I got up. He's not chivalrous at all, he's keeping his berries to himself. Did Rebecca win the bet?"

"Yep"

"Good for her. That will teach him to hide things from me. So, Sherry, what's the plan now? Most fleets will be gone by the evening and we'll be alone in this boring system with nothing to do but babysit a poisonous planet and a defense system that can easily protect it."

151

"Poisonous? Where did you get that report?"

She hands me a data pad with the info of the main planet, what was once the heart of the Conranian Empire, and there it is plain and simple. The toxins on the planet would be enough to kill most humans within a second or two, and most other beings not long after that. But that was before we had the armor suits and the technician to make them space worthy.

"Good thing we just got the first delivery of battle suits and that our mad scientist in engineering is cooking up a way to make them space and poisonous planet worthy."

"Well, isn't that good planning. Now, how are we going to make Hank pay for hiding a stash of fresh strawberries from us?"

11

Chapter 11

It took three days for Augustine to modify the suits and the results I have to admit are incredible. She insisted on testing the technician model herself so I did the same with the marine model and Hank got to test the modified Fernonian model. She had to scrap two more suits to be able to make one perfectly fitted to my bodyguard, a now very sorry he hid fresh strawberries from his love and his commander bodyguard. He is now much the wiser and fresh out of strawberries. After a successful test in the loading bay where we let out all the air and walked around in vacuum in the safety of our ship, it was time for a real test.

Augustine flies the attack shuttle in for a landing on what looks like a normal planet with a normal atmosphere outside the front windows, but looking at the readings on the instruments tells another story all together. Only the three of us came down here and I'm having second thoughts about the whole mission, but I need to trust Augustine's talents and as soon as the shuttle touches down, I walk to the hatch only to be blocked off by my giant friend.

"I will go first. Do not open the hatch if something goes wrong, just leave me."

"Hank, Elena would kill me if I just left you so just hurry so I can get out on my planet. Augustine, you want to wait or are you coming as well?"

"No way I'm waiting in here while you guys have all the fun."

She gets up from the pilot seat after shutting everything down. Just as Hank goes to cycle the hatch to open the outdoor hatch a voice comes inside my head.

'Wait!'

"Hank wait, don't open it yet."

He turns toward me but turns back around as a shadow flow right in front of the hatch window. For the first time I can see real fear in my friend's eyes. I've seen anger and rage, but never fear.

'It is safe now.' The voice comes again.

'Who is this?' I ask.

'Brenda, the system AI. I was given access to every Conranian brain in the system while the Empire existed, and when you made contact upon entering the system, our minds have been linked, as is the person calling himself Chicago.'

'And are you able to contact our people outside of this system once they have established a connection?'

'Yes.'

"Hank, it's safe now."

"Do I want to know Admiral how you know this?"

"System AI Brenda. She talks to me telepathically. The link was created when I accessed the defense system."

"Practical, and invasive at the same time." Hank says as he steps outside.

I follow soon after and then Augustine is last locking the

shuttle up to prevent anything from entering it.

'Brenda, are there any living things out here?'

'I would not call what roams the planet now living, they are more what you would call spirits, of the Conranians that were living here when the biological attack came. The lucky ones died before the attack, but many still lived and now are eternally doomed to roam never to know the peace of death.'

'That was pretty poetic for an AI.'

'I have been alive for many millennia.'

"Admiral, there are shapes floating all over this place." Hank says

"Yes, they are the spirits of the living when the attack came. The poor souls are trapped here for eternity."

"So, Admiral, what exactly are we looking for here?" asks Augustine.

'Brenda, are you able to access our comms?'

'Yes Admiral.'

"Brenda, can you lead us to any technology that could have survived the battle and could help us win the one coming?"

"There are plenty of places on the planet with such technology. Where would you like to start?"

"How about somewhere close by." Hank offers.

"I've never heard of a frighten Fernonian. The race must have gotten soft over the years." Brenda says.

"I am not soft computer." Hank growls.

"That's more like it. Relax Commander I was just pulling your tail."

"I do not have a tail."

"They're still oblivious to humor I see. Please go to the other side of your ship and walk about a hundred feet and you should find rubble that will need clearing for you to access the tunnel.

You should be able to handle that big guy." Brenda says with a smile in her voice.

With a grunt of displeasure Hank takes the lead and soon we find ourselves in front of the rubble Brenda mentioned about and soon, with the help of our suit servos and Hank's incredible strength the tunnel beyond is visible. With some hesitation from all three of us I decide to be the brave one and lead the way inside, the slick rock floor trying to throw us on our butt, but the suit anti-slip soles prevent the floor from winning this round.

The tunnel goes down for several kilometers and finally we come to the end only to be blocked by a door that would give bank vault doors the brush off. About ten feet high and twelve wide with each end entering the rock surface of the ground. No seem can be seen but I doubt Brenda would lead us to our doom so there must be a way in. Just as I am about to ask her how to open the door a loud crack resonates inside the tunnel and right next to me a section of the rock moves outward and I find myself looking at a much smaller tunnel.

"Brenda, is the large metal door even a door at all?" I ask.

"No, just a piece of metal thicker than a ship's haul, with it extending five feet inside the rock on each side."

"Why?"

"Let's ask the engineer in the group. Augustine, what did you think upon seeing the piece of metal?"

"That it would probably take a plasma torch a week to get through that."

"Commander Ionicci, your thoughts?"

"That I would love a portable Gauss rifle at the moment to get through that door."

"And for the benefit of your crew Admiral."

"Right, cause you can read my mind. I was thinking that there must be a way to open the door even if we did not see a seem."

"Three very intelligent officers and none of you thought to look elsewhere then at the piece of metal. That is the purpose of it, to confuse people long enough for the people working inside to escape."

I walk inside the small tunnel and soon find myself turning in the same direction we had been walking before the fake door. Not long after the tunnel opens up into a small room dotted with holes. Before I can ask what this place is Hank answers.

"Kill room."

"That is correct Commander. Anyone coming through here uninvited will find themselves under a barrage of blaster fire so intense that no amount of armor will save them. Of course, you three have nothing to fear."

With that a door opens at the other end and we find ourselves in another tunnel but this one only about twenty feet and it opens into an enormous room. Lights suddenly come on and even with most of the lights still working I cannot see the end of the room. But the most impressive part about the room is what's in it. As far as the eye can see are weapons, vehicles and all manner of equipment I cannot even phantom what they do. I turn my head to look at my two friends and Hank has his eyes locked on the weapons while Augustine is itching to go check out the a fore mentioned no clue what they do equipment.

"Brenda, we are safe here?" I ask.

"As long as you do not remove your suits you will be. I'm not sure who drew up the plans for them but they are much better quality than anything scavengers have brought in the past, to their demise I might add."

"Thank you." I say. "Wait, you let scavengers in the system but you attacked us?"

"The defense parameters are set to attack any ship carrying numerous weapons. As most smaller freighters do not have many weapons, they are able to enter the system."

"Do you have records of all the equipment inside this room?"

"Yes, I do Admiral, this one and the other five like it. As you are the only living heir to the Throne you are privy to this information. I will send them to your comm pad…"

"What?"

"I was saying that I will send…"

"No, I mean what's this about me being the heir to the Throne part?"

"Do you really think the dream you had all those weeks ago when your powers came to you was just a dream? That was a memory from your long-lost ancestor Princess Zoe Brookes. She was third in line for the Throne when the attack came. She died in it but her daughter was with her father on his ship as part of a training exercise for cadets in the Empire Navy."

The other two have barely heard a word of this or they are simply not showing any interest as it is a personal moment for me.

"How can I be of Royal blood? I was born on a small world in the slums of that planet."

"You were born there to protect you. Many will still kill you on sight just for being Conranian. If you need more proof of who you are, only members of the Royal family develop powers. Your friend Chicago will never get them. Yes, he could communicate with me and his ancestry give him superior quickness and agility, but he will not have lifesaving powers like you have. I must say that yours are quite impressive. I am capable of accessing the memories of the members of your crews and from what I see your power exceeds any ever recorded. No one has ever been able to destroy a ship like that."

"It was only part of a ship."

"Yeah Admiral, part of a ship that was still bigger than most of our ships." Augustine offers without being asked.

I smile at her comment. I hate being the center of attention but I love the fact that my crew will stop at nothing to make me feel good, even if it is with a small jab here and there.

"Augustine, instead of your snippy remarks, do you know of a way to get all of this and the equipment at the other locations up to our ships and to a secure location?"

"I do, but it will take some time. I have five other suits I haven't worked on yet so I can use them for techs and we can use the cargo shuttles to get all this equipment up to the *Hand of God*. It's barely ten percent full so we could fit most of what's in here and get it someplace safe. Brenda, any suggestions?"

Augustine seems to be getting familiar with the AI and her confidence in herself grows every time she has an enormous task at hand. I leave her to talk to Brenda and move toward the weapon section. Hank is further ahead looking at the larger weapons but something close by grabs my attention.

Most people would not stop at this section of the weapons display as most prefer blasters than anything up close and personal, except maybe the Xirtans. Most of the swords displayed are rusted beyond repair, or at least I think they are but my expertise in the matter is quite low. My eyes hit on a staff about my height, made of wood and worn smooth from regular rubbing against hands. Ruins run the length of it like a snake twirling around its next victim.

I grab it lightly and even through my suit I can feel my power reacting to the staff. I look around to see if the other two noticed something but both are still doing the same thing never giving me a second look. The staff seems to be edging me to grab one of the rusted swords. I'm not sure what good it will do but I do it anyway as I doubt anything bad can happen. I look at all the ones closer to me, there are hundreds in total, and a smaller slender blade takes my fancy so I reach for it and the second my armored fingers touch it a bright flash of light blinds me for a second until the suit view screen compensates. The light continues on the line of rusted weapons and even to the other weapons. Suddenly power surges inside me like when I destroyed the ship, but the staff seems to be guiding the power instead of letting it flow out in one large cone. Once the power has restored all the items in this room, which is what I understand it just did, the staff urges me to channel it to the tunnel and to give it all I've got. I turn around and face the small tunnel and point the staff in that direction letting the power free itself from me. The concentrated beam flies off into the tunnel and I can actually feel it fly out of it and into the atmosphere. Slowly the power changes and attacks the poison in the air and on the ground closest to the tunnel. Once that's done it flows outward in a circle and pulls more and more power.

I know that if I let go of the staff with this much power I will burn to a crisp, so I keep a tight grip on it and push my mind into the beam to sense what it is doing. It takes over two hours but at long last the power surge inside me stops and I slump to the ground still gripping the staff. I know what's happened but I still cannot believe it. I can no longer feel the power inside me, but if this action has burnt it out of me, it is worth it. I suddenly have the urge to breathe fresh air so I take my helmet off to the cries of both Hank and Augustine, but to their surprise I do not suffocate, I simply breathe clean fresh air. The staff used my power to purify the planet, my planet.

"Well, I guess we don't need to move all this stuff anymore." Augustine says as she also takes her helmet off.

12

Chapter 12

"Admiral, what the hell did you do this time?" asks Captain Elena Ross.

"What makes you think I did anything Captain?" I reply.

"Oh, I don't know, a blinding light and a miracle happening are kind of your signatures."

"You're funny you know that?"

"Tell it to that large rock close to you cause he doesn't seem to find me funny at all. He needs to get a sense of humor that one."

"That he does."

I go on to explain everything that's happened after we landed on the planet. It takes me much longer than it should have because Elena insisted on plugging the rest of the captains halfway through so I had to start all over again. They also kept asking questions. Finally, I gave up and asked Brenda a question that would save us time.

"Brenda, is there a place where twelve shuttles can land close by?"

"There is such a place Admiral."

"Please send the coordinates to all the captains and then the directions to come here."

"Done Admiral."

"Thanks Brenda, you're a life saver."

Brenda doesn't say anything to that but I get a sense of someone smiling in my head.

"Captains, please assemble a small landing party to accompany us. Make sure your head of security is among them and I need either the captain or the first officer to be on the bridge at all times. Everyone will have plenty of time to visit as this will become our home world. Oh, and one more thing, the spirits of the dead are still on the planet roaming around. I don't feel danger from them but..."

Before anyone can ask more questions, I cut the connection. That should make some of the captains less eager to come down right away.

The next few weeks go by like the wind as most people have come down at least once and I now have a team going all over the planet trying to figure out how much housing is available, how much we have to rebuild and finding space for the families of all my crews. With about twenty thousand crew members it already costs me a small fortune to keep fed and safe, so adding at least one more person per crew will bankrupt me for sure. I will need a source of money far greater than the ones Alvaro and Angela will bring in.

'Sherry, you are the heir to the Throne you know.'

'I do Brenda, but how does that help me with this problem?'

Brenda talking to me telepathically has become a regular thing and I always feel I have a friend to talk to.

'You consider me a friend Sherry?'

'Of course, I do. You are always there for help, or if I need someone to run some ideas over with.'

'None of the old Conranians saw me as other than a computer.'

'Well, they were idiots.'

'Thank you. Now for your money problems, the Conranians had a treasury far superior to anything Governments today could dream of having.'

'How much are we talking about here? Just a large amount please, I don't need specifics yet."

'Several hundred trillions in today's credit system.'

'Well, there goes that problem. I've told you before and I'll say it again, you are a life saver Brenda.'

'I try Sherry. Do you want me to contact Geraldine and talk numbers with her?'

'Yes please, and mention to her that she will need a whole team under her and to start taking applicants.'

Just in time LC Stock arrives with some much-needed information.

"Hi Ben, how did the recon go?"

"Not bad Sherry. First the housing, there are plenty of houses and other types for all the crews and their families, even if you allow extended families to come. The ten major cities are in bad shape, especially in the industrial parts. It will take years to rebuild if we have the money, equipment and manpower to do so."

"Money won't be a problem and I saw some construction equipment in one of the six vaults. As for manpower, we can always check with the crews if they have family members that work in that field. What else?"

"Thanks to you cleansing the planet, the fields all over the planet have actually started blooming. I saw a few sprouts of vegetables and fruit trees all over. I even tried an apple that I had the scanner check before and it was one of the best I've ever tasted."

"Any strawberries?" I ask laughing.

Ben looks at me funny but answers in the affirmative. Wait till I tell Rebecca. She might want to be posted down here permanent.

"Did you find a good place for your troops to set up and to grow?"

"The location of the second spaceport would be perfect. The main spaceport close to here could keep its calling while we convert the second one into a military base and it could act as an emergency spaceport if the need arose. The city close to it could be commandeered for the troops and their families, and the factories there could build the ammunition we need as well as vehicles and anything we could need."

"That sounds like a good plan Ben, make it so. Check in with Brenda for all your needs as it might already exist on planet. How are we at getting all the families here on planet?"

"I've sent word out to all the ship's Captains to ask them if their crews wanted their families over here or not, but with the distance it will take some time to get a response."

"I might be able to help in that Lieutenant-Colonel." Interjects Brenda.

"I'm all ears Brenda."

"As part of my protocol I install a tracking device on every ship that comes through this system, including the Admiral's fleet. This device not only tracks the ship's location, but it can use the sensors, communication device and internal systems. In essence, I have also instantaneous communications with all our ships. I am allowed to say our ships Admiral, am I not?"

"You're as much a part of The Red Widow Group as I am or Ben here."

"Thank you, Admiral. I will send your message Lieutenant-Colonel through this system and should have an answer for you shortly."

"I love having an AI on board with us." Ben says as he moves away.

I'm about to head to the administrative building, which is the old library for now and Brenda comes back into my mind, an edge to her voice.

'Sherry, the Alliance is under attack!'

'What do you mean?'

'One of the freighters I've been tracking for a long time now just got destroyed, but I was able to get readings on their fairly good sensors before they were vaporized and a fleet of four hundred plus ships are heading toward the Alliance.'

'Are the fleets in position yet?'

'They will all be before the armada arrives Admiral.'

'Send word to them to be on alert and all the info you can give them. The fleets stationed around a system are to stay at the system itself and protect it at all cost. You can send the other four fleets where you believe they will have the most effect against the armada. Also send word out to Alliance High Command. They will not believe you but we will have worn them. Send a message to Fernon and Peace as well.'

'What about the other corporate fleets Admiral?'

'Advise them as well. But advise both the corporate HQ and every single ship's Captain. If they are worth half the talent needed to become Captain, they will not only protect the installations but the population of their systems.'

'On it. What of here Admiral?'

'I'll take care of the fleet here. Brenda, is there a way for me to access the network you have set up so I can monitor the fleets as they go into fighting?'

'There is Admiral, but the few that have tried have gone insane after a few minutes. It scrambles the brain in many directions and the only way to make sense of it and keep your sanity is to see it all separate. Sounds simple but none have been able to do it. That is part of the reason they created me.'

'My people will be dying out there Brenda, I need to try.'

'I'll send you the information in your mind on where it is and I'll prepare the defense system.'

This fight comes too early, we need more time to bring up the forces. I get the image of a small building close to the mountains and head for a vehicle as I give orders for the upcoming fight.

13

Chapter 13

The assault on my brain comes instantly after plugging of sorts. Thousands of images, data scrolls and sensor inputs come at once and I can easily understand why the people trying to do this go crazy. If not for the determination to see my people through this battle I would probably already be crazy.

I focus my thoughts the way Brenda made me practice before entering the system. Although the enemy have timed their attacks to come at the same time if we go by information Brenda has gathered from other ships, I can only focus on one region at a time or my brain will start mixing the data and I will not be helping my crews but hindering them.

In case something does happen to me Brenda has requested I record all I do; it could also help in future encounters with this enemy. She says that for the recordings it helps to think of each encounter separately so people watching it later can see a single encounter at the same time. So, for recording purposes I will do as she says as the main goal of it is to help my Captains later on.

A few minutes before the battle for Alexandria, I communicate with Brad first to see his status.

"Hey Brad, how are things moving along?" I ask.

It takes a few seconds of silence before Brad says.

"Is that all the message says. This conversation will take days to complete."

"Actually Brad, this is live, so should be quick."

"What the hell Admiral, how are you able to communicate live from home base?"

"Long story and we don't have time. I'll try to help as much as possible from here, and trust me I can help. I have the enemy arriving in about ten minutes. Are you all set up?"

"How... You know what, I'll take you at your word. Yes, all the ships are fully stocked and ready for action. You wouldn't happen to have a composition of their ships, would you?"

"Looks like forty-three ships, mostly heavies. I don't have any data on their weapons yet."

"Oh shit, we're fucked. Sorry Admiral."

"Listen up Captains, you will be facing a force of forty-three heavies mainly, unknown strength and weaponry. Like Brad Sillens said you might think you're fucked, but on the contrary. He has plenty of confidence in you and so do I. Now enough talking, make them regret the day they decided to attack our people."

"Admiral, Captain Conor Sheridan here. Are you the one that sent us the information on which jump point the enemy would be arriving?"

"I am Captain Sheridan."

"How?"

"Let's just leave it at Conranian Tech for now and once all of you are back home, I'll explain everything.

Alright Captains, get into position. Entry in thirty seconds.

Brad, was Alvaro able to repair some of the ships we left behind?"

"Not yet Admiral."

I check the sensors of all the ships and see all of them are hidden in the asteroid belt used mostly for mining. The enemy probably intends to use the asteroid as interference of their entry. This jump point is one of the most dangerous ones in all of the Alliance as it moves regularly, so the pilots coming in through here have to be excellent. All the ships have no other obstacle in their way besides the asteroid hiding them, so as soon as the enemy starts appearing all twenty-five ships move as one out of hiding and fire everything they have at the first ten ships that appear. It does not matter if they have better weapons if they cannot use them. The lasers hit instantly and do some damage, but the dozens of Gauss rifle rounds hitting the ships simply tear them to pieces before they know what is happening.

The hundreds of missiles fired will never reach the ships in time to do any good, but none of them are sent their way. All missiles are fired just behind the first arriving ships where the others pop out just as the missiles arrive. The fireballs this barrage creates is spectacular and several other ships disappear from the screens. The rest of the second wave disperses and open fire as well. The surprise is over, now to let the captains do what they do best.

Of the forty-three that entered the system a few minutes ago only twenty-eight survive and some of those are badly damaged. Now is the time for me to play around the ships while the rest do their work. The recording device in the home system continues to record not only what I do but all information coming from every ship. One of my ships gets hit by several barrage of missiles coming from different ships and the ship simply stops being in my mind. My first instinct is to cry for the lost souls of my crew, but twenty-four other ships need my help.

Something from the last burst of information coming from the downed ship itches at my brain and I take a millisecond to scroll through it and find what it is. The largest ship that attacked it has to be the leader's ship, as it has markings none of the others have. This one arrived in the second wave so it is damaged but functional. But instead of heading back into battle it blasts its reactors to full and heads for the mining station. If they get hold of that station Alvaro won't be able to produce the power suits, and the enemy will have not only the plans but whatever is ready and has not shipped out yet.

I look at the sensors to try and find one of my ships that could pursue and have a chance at stopping that enormous ship, but all are too busy. Another of my ships goes silent and my heart breaks in silence. The sensors tell me that my ships have not gone down without a fight. Of the twenty-eight that survived the surprise at entry, only twenty are left. The only ships now free to go after the leader are on the other side of the battle and will never get there in time. I hate to do this but I need to contact Alvaro.

"Alvaro, are you on the comms?"

"I am Sherry. I wasn't aware you were with the fleet protecting us."

"I'm not, long story. You've got one of the biggest ships I've ever seen coming for the factory. I'm trying to divert some ships there but I won't get there in time. Any weapons on that factory to slow this piece of shit down until my ships can get there?"

"We have better than that Admiral." Replies a voice I don't know.

Suddenly three icons appear from behind the largest asteroid in this sector. It takes hours, or probably more like a second, for the sensors of the closest of my ship to scan the ships and reveal they are three of Alvaro's cargo ships given to him in the transaction.

"Alvaro, call back these ships, they are not equipped to deal with that large of a warship."

"I never sent them Sherry."

"Admiral, you not only gave us an excellent new boss but you gave him the tools to help make life on Alexandria much better for everyone. It's time we give a little back. Me and the other two Captains have already made our decision Admiral, and nothing will stop us. Heavy transports out. Farewell Admiral and good hunting."

The sensors show that they are on an intercept course with the warship. What can they do with only medium blasters and a few large ones to ward off bandits? They have armor but not nearly enough for anything except... ramming the ship.

"Brad, send two ships after that large one heading for the factory."

"Which two Admiral, we're all very busy with the rest of the fleet."

"The transport ships are going to ram the warship in the hopes of stopping it. They don't have enough armor to survive the crash. Their giving their lives away without any hope of survival."

He stays silent for a few seconds until I hear him talking to two ship Captains. The two ships veer off from their encounter and head at dangerous speed toward the warship. The ships they were attacking mean to follow but Brad's ship closes the gap and takes over the pounding the others had been giving.

The main battle is slowly coming to a close as our ships are taking less damage and delivering more, concentrating more on the missiles and Gauss rifles, the weapons that seem to make the most damage. I concentrate on my two racing ships and calculate the odds of them making it on time to save the transports but they are not good.

Not good, that is until one of the pursuing ships fires the two forward mounted Gauss rifles it has. I look at its displays and find that he has shot the last two rounds of its large weapons and doesn't have much more missiles left. The other ship has a few rounds left of missiles but no Gauss rifle rounds. The two Captains should have told Brad they are not equipped to face such a large opponent, but like all the other crews in our ships all they care about is giving everything they can for the mission to be complete.

The duo of Gauss rounds has the desired effect of slowing the warship down so it can face its two smaller adversaries. This will be a massacre and there is nothing I can do but watch. Both smaller ships decide to go for broke and fire all their missiles as soon as the ship comes into range. The warship's defense system takes care of most of them but a few hit with little damage. The massive ship fires to kill with dozens of large blasters and numerous missiles. The two smaller ships evade a lot of the attack but still get hit by many of the missiles. The ship with the Gauss rifle suddenly goes silent and the damage on the other one might have crippled a lot of ships but the captain still keeps it together and fires everything he has.

I look for the transports and all three are a minute out from their ramming action. My ship will never last that long. I know it's wrong to wish for the death of someone to save my crew, but that will be the only thing that could save them now. Several of my other ships are on their way now but won't make it in time. Then a small ship appears close to the station and flies at breakneck speed toward the warship. Jumping in system outside of the jump points is extremely dangerous and stupid but this pilot doesn't seem to mind as he opens his engines to full and flies faster than anything I've seen before except for... Chicago!

The data from the new ship comes in at the same time as my realization. Blaster after blaster, missiles and Gauss rounds spit out of the large fighter and every single one hits the armor of the enemy ship. It turns to face its new annoyance but cannot get a lock on it as he flies faster than any other ship and continues his barrage of destruction all the time. The small ship adds its own blasters to the battle but all both are doing is pissing the captain off, as even if Chicago is doing serious damage, that ship can take it and much more. I need to make hundreds of ships like Chicago's for the fleets.

In all my excitement I forgot to look at the progress of the three transports. I look just in time to see all three hit the large ship at full speed. Chicago and the Captain of the small ship blast the other way to evade the shock wave from the exploding ship. I tap into the small ship's sensors and can see all three transports now fully inside the warship and they add their explosions to the mix.

The fireball barely lasts a second as the air escapes into space, but it is impressive anyway. Chicago heads full speed toward the retreating enemy ships and Brad comes on the line.

"Admiral, permission to follow Chicago and destroy the enemy ships before they make jump?"

All the ships have already powered up and all are heading in that direction.

"You're already heading there, but you would have gotten it anyway Brad. None get away this time."

"Yes ma'am."

All ships push to full power and fire all they have at the seven retreating ships. Chicago does a single pass hitting each ship with a barrage of weapon's fire before disappearing into jump space. Brenda probably sent him telepathically. I will have to thank her.

I take the count of my fleet at this time since only sixteen of my ships give pursuit, some quite slowly I might add. Of the nine left at the battle site, four are completely gone with little chance of finding anyone from those ships alive. Another five have critical damage with several parts of the ships open to space. Casualties on those five will be high, but the majority I hope will be alive and able to come back to their ship once repaired.

Of the sixteen ships destroying the remains of the enemy fleet, all have a degree of damage ranging from extremely heavy to heavy. They took a major hit with this battle but I am happy we came out on top and the facilities and citizens of Alexandria are safe, for now.

14

Chapter 14

The battle for Peace has a major difference in that the Canadian colony already has their own fleet of ships that are in excellent condition and numerous. Led by Hailey Jackson, their fleet of fifteen ships has always been capable of defending their home world and their friendly neighbors. Now their task will be much greater than what they have faced as a full armada of a hundred ships is heading their way. Fortunately, they are a mix of ship sizes, so some will be easier to kill hopefully.

I send a Priority One message to Stephanie Blanche to head there as fast as possible. Now I need to check in with Julie on how the preparations are coming along.

"Hi Julie, how are the preps going?" I ask after the usual 'how is it that we are live' talk.

"Good Admiral I believe. I'm not a Captain or anything so my knowledge of space battles is limited, but we seem to be ready for anything."

"So, you're twenty-five and their fifteen are ready to take on a hundred ships the enemy is sending your way?"

"I'm sorry Admiral, I thought you said a hundred ships."

"I did Julie. Let's patch in the captains and we can talk about this all together."

Once all twenty-five Captains as well as Julie is on line, I use the comms from Julie's ship to patch in Hailey so she will have all the information as well.

"Listen up people. We show an armada of about a hundred ships heading for your system. I believe their goal is to cripple the Alliance's capability to heal itself by taking out one of their best healer planets. To prevent any questions, yes, we have confirmation that all hundred are heading your way. I know Fernon is close as well but they also have a fleet of enemy ships heading there to finish the job started several weeks ago.

From what we're able to determine the enemy have at least eight targets in Alliance territory, so resources are thin. I'm doing my best to try and get you some reinforcements before they arrive but the chances are thin. Hailey, anything you care to say that could help raise morale a bit?"

"Actually, I do Admiral. Several years ago, we had a Corp force try and take over our system for our medical tech. We had a much smaller ship fleet at the time but thanks to a convoy of Brandari ships arriving at the right moment to take delivery of some equipment we were able to defeat the corps. At that time, we bought more ships and created a special surprise for any fleet entering our system uninvited."

"Is that why you mentioned us coming to your Prime Minister after Fernon?" I ask.

"It is Admiral. All across the system, close to the jump points, we have defense mines that are placed all over. When we have positive identification of the ship or ships coming in, we deactivate the mines and they simply move away from the ships flying in. They are micro nuclear mines, which means they pack a punch even if they barely are the size of a ball."

"Well, that's good to know. Glad to be friends Captain. So, Captains, this is what I suggest."

After explaining the plan, the ships disperse all over the jump points until five minutes before the enemy gets here and we are able to figure out that they are coming from six points of entry. The fleet rushes to place themselves 'in front' of the jump points at a distance greater than the enemy's known weapon range. As soon as the ships start appearing the defenders, with numbers against them two and a half to one, start flying back to the planet with their tails between their legs. At least that's what it looks like to the enemy.

As soon as the enemy ships jump in and see our ships fleeing, they send their smaller and faster ships full speed after us. That is their first mistake as the lead ships all of a sudden seem to vaporize into thin air, or no air in this case. Several of the larger ships are already well on their way to full speed so slowing down is not an easy task. A couple of them do not make it to a full stop before the mine field and follow their smaller brothers to meet whatever God they worship.

The mine field has two effects on the enemy. The first is obvious and devastating to them, but the second is as useful to us as the first one: They can't move. None of the ships can spot the mines or scan them, so none of them have a clue where they are if any are left. Hailey gave us the codes to scan their location and numbers and from what I can gather most of the mines have been detonated. We know this, but they do not. The mines are able to be turned on and off, but they can also move in space with tiny propeller engines not visible to radar. Hailey showed me how to work them since I had no way of affecting the battle.

All of the Widow ships and their Peace friends turn back right after the explosions and are now firing from maximum range, doing more damage to the ships left at each jump point. A few ships from four groups brave up and advance past the mine fields, or so they think. As soon as they pass the point where the mines had been I send a couple mines into each ship close to the engine compartments. The mines basically depleted, I send word to the fleets that they're on their own from now on.

From a hundred ships that entered the Peace system only sixty-two are left, but these look mean and are barely damaged. To the fleets credit they split up into smaller groups and speed up toward the enemy. I notice that all the groups have both Widow ships as well as Peace ships. I'll have to send the Canadian fleet a few of the ships similar to Chicago's when they are built. I send a message to Brenda to start on the plans for the factory for them as well as for larger warships. We'll need them in the years to come.

The slug fest has started as the enemy ships realize none of the mines are left. Right now, most of the shots are hitting shields but that will change quickly on both sides. I check the status of Stephanie's fleet but can't find them anywhere. Could they have been destroyed somehow by an enemy fleet we did not see? I look at the last known location for them if it gives me any clue. The last location for every ship in her fleet is where they were when I sent the message. I see that all of them jumped out of the system and then all of them winked out of existence. Could the tracker that Brenda placed on each ship have fallen off of all the ships at the same time?

I write to Brenda to ask how this could be explained. She writes back that she has noticed that over the hundreds of years she has been scanning ships. She goes on to tell me that she attaches the transmitter to the IFF transmitter on the ships since it is always broadcasting. That explains it then. Stephanie had her ships shut theirs down to prevent the enemy from knowing they were coming. The IFF stands for Identification of Friend or Foe. By law every ship in the Alliance has to have this equipment working and activated. You can face serious jail time for deactivating it, but I believe we can pardon Stephanie for this one time.

The problem now is I have no way of knowing when she will arrive to help Peace make it out of this battle. Brenda sends a message that the plans for the ship factory are done. I love having an AI to work with. She has tasked the many robots she controls on the home world to start construction and to use any materials they would need. She has also sent a message to Alvaro that they will need to up the production of the new material by a thousand percent. Angela has also received a message with equipment that will need building at her factories.

All that happened in the space of a second which would blow my mind normally but seeing how I can travel from one ship to another in an instant, not much surprises me anymore.

One of our ships suddenly takes some serious damage and makes a run for the planet to try and stay alive. As one the ships around it, both Widow and Peace, block off any further attack from touching it but pay dearly for it. Two more ships are heavily damaged but able to stay in the fight. All of a sudden, the ship heading for Peace is coming back into the fight, shields all concentrated forward and its engines to full power. The defenders get out of the way just in time to prevent being hit but the enemy ships are not that lucky and the Widow ship fires everything it has right in the middle of them and then just as its shields give way slams into the biggest ship in the enemy group. To my sadness, the Widow ship explodes with none of her crew making out alive, or did they?

Halfway to the planet I can scan dozens of lifeboats making a run to Peace. I scan the information about the ship before its demise and find only five percent of the regular complement aboard, most flying the ship or firing the weapons. The wall of heroes back home will be enormous at this rate.

The kamikaze actions of our ship have the desired effect and the enemy hesitates. This only lasts for a few seconds but it's enough for the rest of the ships to take advantage of this and fire all they have at the rest of the ships. Out of the seven ships left after the collision, four more explode in the seconds after by concentrated fire from the ships. The enemy Captains now knows it is under gunned and try to leave, but they barely start turning before they join their fellow ships in oblivion.

I look at the other five battle 'grounds' and find that two more ships have done the same ramming action to save lives, both ejecting most of their crew before taking out an important target. Four freighters stuck in Peace space are already on their way to collect the life boats of all three ships.

Suddenly an enemy ship barely flying still wants to imitate his enemies and tries to ram one of the Peace ships, but comes across a wall of missiles and Gauss rounds that pulverize it to space dust. After this most of the enemy ships left try to regroup for a final attack, and with still superior numbers it just might work. Suddenly twenty-five ships appear out of thin air near the enemy's position and poor so much firepower into them that not one of them has time to react. The fireworks are impressive if short lived.

All twenty-five IFFs come on and it confirms what I already know, that the 8th fleet has arrived. I'm happy that no one else is dead but this took way too long. I will have to find a solution to this soon.

"Thanks, Stephanie, for the timely arrival, but I fear I cannot let you celebrate with the rest of the Peace delegation as Rjoart needs your help badly with his plan. I swear this man has a death wish."

"Will do Admiral. Fleet let's move out."

"Admiral, we'll follow fleet eight to Fernon." Julie says on the line.

"You will do no such thing and that's an order. Peace also lost several ships and I want to make sure they are well protected until they can repair."

"But we can still help Admiral."

"Of that I have no doubt Julie, but your fleet has done something I've never seen before in Alliance space, work in perfect harmony with the Peace fleet. Consider this your posting from now on. As for the rest of the Captains, I hope you do not mind being posted here as well?"

"None of us would leave if given the choice Admiral." One of the Captains says.

"Excellent."

"Another detail before you leave Admiral. I would like to propose Miss Fortin be raised as Commodore and permanently in charge of third fleet. She has proven herself resourceful in this battle and although she has some crazy ideas sometimes, they turn out to be excellent at saving people's lives."

"Are all of the captains present in agreement with this proposal?"

All are, some quite forcefully as well. They seem to trust her which makes the decision an easy one.

"Julie Fortin, I am giving you the field promotion of Commodore of third fleet. A more formal celebration will follow after all this crap is over. Congratulations Commodore Fortin."

A barely heard thank you Admiral comes from her comm. I agree with the captains as I review the comms during the battle just before I head over to Fernon. She might have lost eight ships and another twelve that have severe damage, but considering that they came into this battle with only a small chance of survival, those numbers are quite good. And of the eight ships destroyed, three of the crews are almost full strength and ready to board a new ship and continue saving the Alliance.

15

Chapter 15

I was hoping the enemy would not send a large force to Fernon so the people I have grown to love so much would be spared another massacre like a few weeks ago, but of course the enemy did not care about my wishes and sent a force of sixty ships to finish what the other fleet had started. They were surely not expecting a fleet of twenty-five warships in perfect condition and I'm doubly sure they were not expecting a small fleet of ten Fernon ships, or more precisely enemy ships converted to fit the Fernonian physiology and language.

It's obvious the Fernon ships are not finished as the paint on them are a collection of every color the enemy has, and I'm pretty sure not all the weapon systems work from what I can gather from the scans, but never under estimate the rock people. They might have a few surprises up their sleeves, or under a crevice might be more precise in their case. The sixty ships enter at the same jump point far from the planet and the defense force. Before advancing they form up and then engage their engines at half power from what I can tell. They are either not in a hurry to fight the people that defeated them the first time or they have something in store and they are stalling for time. That serves us as well as it might give us time for reinforcements.

Unlike all the others, when I comm Rjoart he doesn't ask how I am able to talk to him live from the home world.

"Admiral, they are preparing something big. I have a plan but I need to get off the ship to make it work. Permission to do so?"

"Rjoart, you are in command of this fleet, you make the calls. Talk to your Captain and see what he thinks of it."

"I already did Admiral and he agrees with me."

"Then do so. Captains, as you can see you will be facing a fleet of sixty well-armed ships. You need to work closely with the Fernonians if you stand a chance of defeating them."

"We're not too worried Admiral, Rjoart is on our side. That little Xirtan is capable of miracles." One of the Captains calls out.

"I love the confidence you have in him, and trust me that I have the same confidence as you do, but he is still only a single person."

"Excuse me Admiral, might I interject?" One of the Captains of the Fernonians asked.

I have included them in the conversation to make sure they understand that we are in this together. They are a very proud people.

"You may Captain."

"I might not have said this a couple of months ago, but I agree with your Captains. I was at the palace during the attack, pinned down and under heavy fire. He entered the corridor where I was and ran at the enemy without any armor. A few seconds later there was no weapon's fire coming my way. I had time to lift my head to see him run of into another hot zone. I walked to the enemy that had been firing at me. I counted twelve dead."

"I'm happy he was able to change your views of his people Captain."

"He not only did that Admiral, he also started training some of my people in his way of fighting. He is not going alone on his mission Admiral; he has twenty of the best trained Fernonians with him. They might not be as ferocious as the Heir Prince, but they are close."

If those twenty were anywhere near the skill Hank has, the enemy had better be worried.

Suddenly five small attack shuttles leave the main Widow ship and heading toward the enemy. All of a sudden, the thirty-five ships of the Fernon defense force power up their engines and slowly head toward the enemy. As soon as the main ships catch up to the shuttles they veer off and fly away from the fleet. Is Rjoart going to board the enemy ships and destroy them from inside? That little Xirtan is crazier than I thought, but then again, he did subdue a few ships for me not too long ago.

I patch into the lead shuttle to talk to my little assassin.

"Rjoart, are you planning to kill every single enemy bare handed?"

"That Admiral would be the optimal solution as it would save a lot of people."

"I agree but even with twenty elite fighters with you that task will be impossible. What can I do to make it easier for you guys?"

"Are you able to access their floor plans?"

"Let me check how I can do that."

I send a message to Brenda to see if we are able to do that. She writes back that they must attach to the ship itself and send a laser comm signal to the main ship. At that time I will be able to infiltrate their systems and find some answers. She mentions that this could also be fatal if they have safeguards against such things and suggest that she do it since she has practice against hostile computer systems. I agree but ask her to copy me on the floor plan and to make it possible for me to see the progress the elite fighters are doing.

A few seconds later she comes back with instructions on how to do it for the group of shuttles. I send the information on a laser transmission so the enemy cannot pinpoint Rjoart's location. He then returns a transmission to the main ship with the target ships they will be entering.

"Captain Dubois, what's the plan for not killing our own troops on those ships?"

"We plan on hitting those ships as well so as not to bring too much attention to our troops, but most of what will make it to the ships will be blaster fire. They should be able to sustain quite a bit of those before it becomes a danger for the teams on board."

"And what exactly are they trying to accomplish on there? Killing officers?"

"Ma'am, I've heard rumors about the Xirtan, not having met any before Rjoart, and the leaders of the Fernonian have made the rumors completely useless. The Xirtan are far deadlier than anything I had heard before. So, in other words I never asked what he planned to do and just agreed to anything he said. Anyway, from what I gathered from the same leaders is that he is loyal to you to the core. That's good enough for me."

"Well after this battle Captain he will also be that loyal to all of you. I'll keep you informed as I get info."

"Thank you, Admiral. Dubois out."

The shuttles are close to their targets, now traveling under constant speed, not daring to use their thrusters so as not to give themselves up. The second the enemy ships are in firing range all thirty-five defender ships let go with everything they have for a first volley. As the shuttles get close to the two target ships the fleet fires a single Gauss rifle round at each ship, firing at the other ships as well. The Gauss rounds break up the shields close to the shuttles at the right moment and all five shuttles enter the field and attach to the ships. The fleet pours more and more missiles into the enemy, two of which break apart under the heavy assault.

Suddenly two dots appear toward the rear of the enemy fleet, both being large ships that look ready to take on a lot of damage. I have to give it to the little assassin, he knows how to prepare his troops. Hopefully he'll survive this so he can join his friend Julie in leading this group long term.

I concentrate on the ship where Rjoart enters through a hatch he forces open. Another shuttle accompanies him on the boarding of this ship, the other three shuttles and twelve elite soldiers hit the other ship. Suddenly an image springs to life and I can see the little assassin in front of me.

"Are you getting the feed Admiral?" asked an elite trooper.

"I am, thank you."

"Our leaders wanted us to film our battles to try and bolster the support of the rest of the people for what we do. I thought you might enjoy the same feed but live in your case."

They advance quickly through the ship and I can see that half the group is heading for the bridge and the other half to engineering. They're gonna try to take the ships, are they nuts?

Of course, Rjoart is in the lead. Good thing that Stephanie's fleet is on its way over to lend a hand cause this might not be such a good plan. But what do I know of battles anyway.

I check in on the battle raging outside the ship and find that the defenders, although with an excellent start, are now in danger. The superior numbers of the enemy are starting to show as they try to flank on both sides while the main part of their fleet keeps the defenders busy.

"Captain Dubois, might I suggest sending the *Hellcat* and the *Firewolf* to deal with the flanking threat?"

"Excellent idea Admiral. Comms, send them a message to safeguard our flanks. They are to throw everything they have at those fuckers. Sorry for my language Admiral."

"No need to apologize when it comes to the enemy Captain."

I return to the camera view in time to see Rjoart dispatch three enemy soldiers close to the bridge. For the first time I can see who our enemy is.

Tall, muscular, blueish tint to their skin, long black hair and green irises. They are humanoid in shape and move basically like we do. These are not the same soldiers that attacked Fernon's surface the first time around.

Five of these soldiers block the entrance to the bridge with automatic blasters firing with abandon. Rjoart is about to run at them, probably to his death as well, when two of the Fernonians rush in front of him and block the blaster shots with their thick rocky skin. They are hurting if their screams are any indication, but they don't stop until they run the soldiers over and ram the bridge hatch. The second they hit the bridge they fall to the ground. I can see them still moving so they are alive, but what captures my attention is my friend.

Rare are the moments that I've been able to admire his talent at killing enemies. Twin swords become a blur as they follow his movements in a sort of dance of death. The bodies fall in his wake and the only evidence of his passing is a thin line on the victim's neck, torso, arms or legs, anything that comes in his way of complete destruction.

The elite carrying the camera barely has time to take one enemy out before Rjoart has dispatched the rest. The last enemy has not even touched the floor that the Xirtan sits at the helm and motions for the others to take their position. Cameraman helps the other two up and I can see both their fronts are charred black. They move with pain but move they do. All three head for weapons management and wait for Rjoart's word. He seems to listen to something before he turns to the trio.

"All good, let's have some fun."

I switch to the outside sensors of *Hell's Cradle*, Captain Dubois's ship, and I have front row seats to mayhem. The two targeted ships are now in possession of the defenders and they immediately turn on the surrounding ships, dishing out serious punishment. I look quickly to the flanking ships and they are all caught in a serious battle with both large warships of the Widow group. Now most of the ships the enemy has brought to battle seem confused, as they are being hit from behind but no ships from the opposition seem to be there. By the time they realize what is happening ten of their rear ships have been destroyed.

Then all hell breaks loose as Stephanie and her fleet arrive all around them, arriving close to the battle by Brenda's guidance of the jump points. I quickly send them the information about the two ships we control and ask her to send marines or security teams to clear the ships. The twenty-five pristine ships come in and completely destroy the rest of the fleet of sixty.

The marines soon arrive at the captured ships and the mop up mission starts. As with the other battles I check the damage this battle has cost the group and find only three ships destroyed, while all the rest have a variety of damage. Still, even at a low ship cost, the people on those ships will never be seen again.

Of the ten ships the Fernonians had put together only six remain. All ships fly close to the planet to start on repairs and I get a comm message from the surface thanking me for our assistance.

"It is my pleasure King to help out friends. Now, our joint force captured two complete enemy ships. My forces have suffered casualties but you have suffered as well, twice instead of once. Please take the two ships to help rebuild your forces."

"That is most graceful Admiral, but we cannot accept. Without your forces, we would have once again been wiped out. The ships are yours."

"Well, what if we both took one. Would that be acceptable for you?"

"I believe our friendship will only grow Admiral. Please thank everyone in your fleet for their service."

"Actually King, if you would not mind, I would like them to stay here for a while. The enemy knows you are friends and will want to make us pay by hurting the ones we love. I know that the crews of the first fleet I had when coming here the last time enjoyed their time on planet. If you do not mind the added traffic on your planet, I would like them to become a semi-permanent force in the Fernon system. Once your forces have grown large enough to protect your world, they could become a patrol force based here. Would that be acceptable for you?"

"Would we need to loge them and feed them?"

"No sir, I pay them well enough that they will have to pay for everything they buy, and the ships are their home. So, it would add substantial trade to the surface economy."

"So not only are you protecting us, but you are growing our economy. Admiral, as your people like to say, what's the catch?"

"There is no catch. For now, you need to rebuild and grow your economy so you can strengthen your defense. Once all is back to optimal conditions, we can talk again and see what could benefit both our worlds."

"Admiral, I am glad that you are the person our son says you are. I can almost look past you calling him by his first name. Almost. Good day Admiral."

With that the connection cuts.

"Stephanie, how are your ships doing?"

"I kind of feel bad Admiral. We're the only force that's been in two battles and suffered no loses because we arrived at the end."

"Don't feel bad, you helped at both places. Please set up a patrolling schedule for all your ships, in groups of five, for the surrounding space. I need your fleet there in case both Peace and Fernon need a little extra help."

"Will do Admiral."

Next stop Glengarry.

16

Chapter 16

I hook up with Aaron and his fleet just as they come out of jump space. Once again, a large fleet from the Red Widow Group enters in force the Glengarry system and this time six attack ships fly at breakneck speed toward us. I ask the fleet Captain and Aaron to let me handle it this time.

"Leader of the attack ships coming to welcome us, please be advised that we come to help you protect your planet against a large fleet of enemy to the Alliance from a system we do not know. We are not enemies here guys, we are friends."

"The last time you people entered our system you took half of our ground forces with you. The Council is not very happy."

"There won't be a Council in a few hours unless we defeat the fifty-five warships coming this way."

"What?"

"You heard correctly Captain. Now I notice you have double the attack ships coming our way and another three close to the planet. The first time we came you only had three. I wonder how you got your hands on six more of the rare ships."

This wasn't a question because I know exactly how they got

them. Angela has been using some of the profits to build them for the local Navy, to better protect the planet. These ships are not jump capable but have great armor, speed and weaponry. They can make good allies for the upcoming battle.

"That's none of your business Admiral Lebronski."

"Good, you remember my name. It is my business as I'm the reason you have them. Angela Laurent got the companies from me and most of the money used to build these attack ships comes from products I bought from her. Now you will head back to your regular orbit and we will join you so we can formulate a plan of defense. Is that acceptable to you, or do you have to check with the Council?"

I close the connection and tell all my Captains to move forward toward the planet.

"Aaron, call your buddy and see what he can do about shutting that Council up. We need military people here to defend, not politicians."

"On it, Admiral."

A few minutes later Aaron comes back on the comm.

"Admiral, I have someone that would love to talk to you."

"Could it be the most handsome former guard member ever?"

"You got that right Sherry." Answers Hector.

"It's good to hear your voice my friend."

"Same here Admiral. I thought Aaron said you stayed on Conra V?"

"I am on Conra V Hector. It's a long story and we don't have time right now. Does Angela have any sway with the Council members?"

"Yep, they practically eat out of her hand. The fact that she gives a large portion of the profits to help with schools, defense, infrastructure and a dozen other programs might have something to do with that."

"I knew she was the right person for the job. I need her to have the defense force work with us on the defense of the planet. I'm sure Aaron told you all about the encounter we had on Fernon a few weeks back. Well, their back and hitting us on several fronts. We've got fifty-five warships heading this way and Aaron only has twenty-five warships at his disposal. Nine attack ships would add some serious firepower."

"Ten."

"What?"

"Ten attack ships. I have my very own attack ship with crew and all. And mine has jump capability. Angela built it for me so if she ever needs to go anywhere, she has her own private warship."

"Well, you will be very welcome to join the fight."

"I'll personally lead the attack ships and all of us will report to you Admiral."

"Thanks sweetheart."

"Admiral please, Angela might hear and get jealous."

With that the comm cuts and not long after a ship takes off the surface and joins the others. Soon after they form up behind Hector. I wonder if those attack ships stand a chance against an enemy such as we are facing now. I guess we'll see the results soon enough.

Hector forms a plan of attack with Aaron but the big fellow doesn't like it one bit. He and our ships are to hide behind the nearest moon to the jump point the enemy will be coming in system in and wait for the attack ships to engage them before showing himself. Aaron believes it is pure suicide, but I have a feeling these small ships are more capable than he thinks.

"Aaron, I hate the idea of hiding while Hector and his ships fight it out, but a few things here need to be said before you argue some more. First is that those ships look small and fragile, but the scans show thicker armor than on your biggest warship. They have speed and their weapon compliment is commendable. I hate to say it but my second point is we need to see those ships in action against superior forces so we can evaluate how much they will be able to help in the near future in other systems, and among our ranks even."

"I still hate it Admiral. What if they get killed before we can reach them?"

"Hey big guy, we're faster than anything they have I'm sure of it, so if I see we're in trouble I call in the cavalry and get the hell out of the way. Admiral, any idea when they should be in system?"

"Sorry Hector no. They were on our scanners a few times which makes us sure they are coming here, but last time we spotted them was several hours ago. Earliest they could be here would be in twenty minutes."

"Alright you Italian stud, get your people in position."

"Glad you remember who's the most handsome between the two."

With that Aaron sends his ships to hide behind the moon and wait, and wait some more. An hour later the enemy has not made an appearance yet and I'm starting to get nervous. Could they have bypassed this system to attack another undefended one? I'm about to say something when Hector comes on the comm.

"Contact on the long-range sensors. They should be here in a minute. But Admiral, I only count twenty-four on the scan, not fifty-five."

"Are you waiting on company?"

"Nope ma'am."

The ships emerge into normal space and I'm about to scan them for damage signs, in case they went somewhere else before, but the IFF shows them as Alliance ships.

"This is Commodore Glen Michaels of the Alliance Navy, to what do I owe the greeting of ten attack ships with shields raised and weapons hot? This is a violation of…"

"Can it asshole, we've got fifty-five ships coming in with intent to destroy us. They've already tried on several other systems and met with The Red Widow Group."

"That group of illegal bandits are not allowed to fire any weapons in Alliance Territory without a written authorization from the President himself. I will…"

"You will what Commodore, take them in custody? Their ships outnumber your entire fleet four to one and every single one of them is at least half the age of your youngest ship. They are the only reason right now there IS an Alliance. Now either you get out of our way and leave or you stand behind us and defend one of your worlds."

"How dare you interrupt me like that? What's your name and rank sir?"

"Commander Hector Hernandez, at your service."

"A commander should show respect to a high-ranking officer. I will speak with your superior. I will not tolerate being spoken to by a simple Commander."

"Will an Admiral do?" I ask joining the conversation.

"Who is this?"

"Admiral Sherry-Ann Lebronski, leader and owner of The Red Widow Group. Now I suggest you do what Commander Hernandez has requested because in less than five minutes you will be in the crossfire between the defending force in front of you and fifty-five enemy ships."

"The Alliance does not recognize your group miss Lebronski."

Hector's ship fires a blaster right off the bow of the Commodore's ship, the largest in the Alliance fleet.

"It's Admiral Lebronski Commodore, and don't you forget it again."

"You have just fired at an Alliance ship Commander, that is a capital offense. Captains arrest that man and his ships..."

"Get behind us now!" screams Hector.

At that point several things happened in only a few seconds. Commodore Michaels fires at Hector's ship but it barely rubs against his shields. Hector and his ships fire all they have past the Alliance fleet and hit the incoming enemy ships just as they come out of jump space. The enemy ships also fire as soon as they come in the system and the Alliance ships are right in the middle making them bleed badly. The ships not destroyed outright, like the one the Commodore had been on, open their engines to full power in the hopes of getting to cover. Although I know the plan was for us to wait a bit to join the party, I tell all our ships to go to full power and hit the enemy from the flank instead of the back.

Twenty-five warships come around the moon, all in a different approach, and the second a ship is in their cross hairs they fire all they have. In this battle I want to see what the attack ships, and Hector's jump capable model, can do against such a strong force so I check the sensors and the initial numbers are scary. All the ships are engulfed in blaster bolts and I'm afraid we've already lost them, but then I hear Hector calmly tell his ships a single word: Now.

All of a sudden ten missiles spring away from the blaster show and start doing evasive maneuvers all the while firing all their weapons at ship after ship. The attack ships show all their glory as they head directly in the middle of the enemy ships and fire at close range right into engine bays, weaken parts of the ships where my ships have done some serious damage and even directly into airlocks trying to depressurize the ships.

The ballet is so beautiful that I wonder if a force of a hundred of these could be stopped. I need some of these small ships for every system we protect as well as for the Group fleets. Time for a little business while the Navy guys and girls have fun. I make a few scans and find the ship best equipped for comms to the planet and I call Angela.

"Sherry, where the hell are you? I thought Aaron was in charge of this fleet?" she asks right away.

"He is Angie, I'm on Conra V. Before you ask, it's Conranian tech."

"Wouldn't mind getting my hand on tech like that. How's the battle going?"

"Aren't you checking the scanners?"

"No, too afraid of what could happen to Hector."

"From what I can see the odds are evening out so not bad at all, I guess. The Alliance fleet that came in just before the enemy are actually making a difference now that their pompous ass Commodore is gone."

"What can I do for you Sherry?"

"I need to place an order for fifty of the jump capable ships like Hector's, and a hundred of the regular attack ships. When can you start the order and when can I get them?"

"Whoa, how many systems do you plan on protecting?"

"Actually, the regular ones are just for Conra. The jump

capable ones will replace the destroyed ships in my fleets for now until I can build my own larger ships and then we'll see how I use them."

"A hundred ships to protect just one system? That's nuts."

"Yep, but I don't want a repeat of what happened to my people before. I healed the planet and I intend to keep it healed."

"You what? You know what, never mind, nothing surprises me anymore with you. I can produce two jump capable ones a month and double that on the regular ones."

"I'm afraid that won't be fast enough. I'll transfer you some funds, an advance on the order, so you can grow the plants and hire the people you need. I need the full order filled within a year. Oh, and I almost forgot, several of the systems we protect will be sending you orders as well once they see the vids I'll send them of the initial part of the battle."

"You're a crazy chick Sherry-Ann Lebronski, but I love crazy. Consider it done. What's the advance going to be like? Each regular ship costs twelve million and the jump capable ones cost twenty million."

"I'll send you half the amount of the order."

"Sherry, that's one point one billion credits."

"I know. They'll be in your account by morning. Sorry now I've got to go see how my investments are doing."

With that I cut the comm and look at the sensors again to see how the battle is taking shape. Only twelve of the fifty-five ships are left and only one of the attack ships has been destroyed. The enemy ships are making a run for the jump point but my fleet is there blocking the way and making sure they stay put while Hector's crew and the rest of the Alliance ships mop up the rest of the enemy.

Once all is quiet again a comm comes in from one of the ten Alliance ships left.

"Hello, this is Captain Kevin Anders of the Alliance fleet, could I have a word with Admiral Lebronski please?"

This guy is much more polite, I like him.

"This is Admiral Lebronski Captain Anders, what can I do for you?"

"First Admiral I'd like to apologize for the behavior of the Commodore. Not all of the Alliance commanding officers are like him. Second, I'd like to thank you and you fleets for protecting the systems we cannot protect. We got word of the many other battles your fleet are or has been fighting to protect our people. I cannot promise the Alliance will be able to compensate you for the ships you've lost. As you can see, they can't even get us decent ships. Third Admiral, I've received the same message from all of the Alliance ships left in this system as well as the people on the other ships that are still alive that if you need crews for future ships, we would be honored to resign our commission with the Alliance and join your Group."

Well, that's interesting. I don't want to weaken the Alliance, but then again if these great crews don't have ships to go with it, it becomes a waste of talent. I will need to talk to the head of the Alliance soon.

"Thank you for those words Captain. I do not intend to ask the Alliance for any compensation for the lost ships or their crews, I will take care of them myself. As for you and the rest joining my Group, I would be honored. I will send you my information and if you are able to make sure that your ships are crewed before transferring to us, then I will take any crew member that will conform to our guidelines, that will also be transmitted to you. We may have great ships Captain Anders, but that also means that you will be facing this enemy and others like them on a regular basis. No one in the Group has a cushy job."

"Excellent Admiral, we look forward to receive your information."

With that it's time for the revue of the battle, again. Maybe that's why people go crazy in here, all the death of your comrades. The Alliance lost more than half its force, Hector only lost a single ship but all will need serious time in the repair bays, and the Group lost six more ships. I hope Brenda will be able to set up the ship building factory soon because we will need to reinforce the fleets. Yes, the JCAS, or jump capable attack ships as I'm calling them, will be a big help, but I want to add them to the fleets, not replace larger ships with those.

With five JCAS per fleet, it permits them to be unpredictable and, when on patrol, they could have one per patrol with larger ships and easily come back faster to warn any system. A message from Brenda comes in.

With the JCAS arriving in less than a year, do I bother with the small freighters like Chicago's?

Yes Brenda. Those will be able to patrol the whole Alliance and pass themselves off as freighters. Any trouble comes up they might be able to handle it, otherwise they will be fast enough to get word to their command. The JCAS will be posted with the fleet while the freighters will be independent.

Brenda doesn't answer back because she doesn't need to, she has her answer.

Next is the Kroh system where hell might break loose if the council finds out my friend gave me secret information.

17

Chapter 17

It seemed like the obvious choice at the time to send Diana to protect her home world of Kroh, but as I launch my mind to her ship, I keep getting this feeling of dread, that I made a fatal mistake at the choosing of postings. As soon as I connect with the ship my dread turns to horror. The scanners show the Kroh defense system firing at my ships.

"Diana, what the hell's happening?" I ask.

"My people seem to think I betrayed them and I've been trying to let them know I did so only for the greatest of cause. They don't seem to like my answers."

"If they do not want our help then get out of there. All ships leave the Kroh system at once. Head for the closest system to wait for further orders."

"But Admiral, the enemy is at their doorstep."

"I know that Diana, but I cannot save people that do not want our help. As soon as you hit normal space at the system I just sent you the coordinates to, I will contact you. Make sure you are on a secure line at that moment."

As soon as the ships prepare to leave, I use the link to drop a sensor drone to stay in the system. Even though I said I could not help them, I will not let their planet suffer the same fate as Conra V did all those years ago. The ships all jump out of the system fairly intact and the trip to the next system feels like months in the computer system but only takes about thirty minutes. Diana enters her quarters and sits at her station.

"Sorry Diana for placing you in your home system, I should have thought about the fact that I know what I know. I didn't know the range of their ability and thought you would be fine in space."

"If they would only be singular people then yes, I would have been fine, but the defense system is used by combining twenty minds together. They are the ones that felt my betrayal and reported it. That is when the defense system fired on us and did not stop."

"Did any of the ships return fire?"

"No, Captain Fisher was quick to order that no ship fire on the defense system or the planet. They could only evade or destroy missiles."

"Excellent. I dropped a sensor drone in the system before you left. That should give you enough information to make a decision when the enemy arrives. Once our conversation finishes ask Captain Fisher to move the ships just outside of sensor range of the system. As soon as the enemy appears in the system the drone will tell you and you can make a decision at that moment. Again, Diana I am sorry to have placed you in this situation."

"That's OK Sherry, the Council still think themselves in the dark ages when every ship was a threat."

The fleet soon transfer to a minute's travel out of the Kroh system and I start scrolling through the data from the drone.

All is quiet at the moment which makes me nervous. A comm comes in from Brenda Vixon, fleet five commander and my second floater fleet for which I have not had any use yet.

"Admiral, I'm requesting permission to head to Rockwall to help out a Corp system that are faced with one hell of a problem. The enemy is more than twice their size and contrary to most Corp Captains, Aunt Martha cares more for the people than for the Corp."

"Aunt Martha?"

"She asks everyone to call her that instead of Captain. In her eyes all the people under her command are family."

"I like her already. How far are you?"

"We should be there in five minutes Admiral."

"So, you're asking permission as a formality since you've been going there for a while now."

"Yes Admiral, sorry Admiral."

"Never be sorry to want to help people. A little more advance warning next time might be appreciated. Give them hell Brenda."

"Admiral, sensors detect fifteen ships arriving at the Kroh system in less than a minute." Diana says.

"Fifteen, that's it?"

"Yes Admiral. From memory the defense system should have no problem dealing with them."

"I don't like it, Diana. Spread your ships out to cover all the jump points and let me know what you find. Have them search further out, maybe up to thirty minutes from the system."

"You think the fifteen are a decoy Admiral?"

"Maybe not but at the least only a first wave."

Diana gives the orders and the ships spread out to jump to different locations where another enemy force could be waiting. We really need to find a name for these people. Calling them enemies is too general, the Alliance needs to have a name to focus their anger at as well as their efforts. Jump after jump the ships search in groups of five and send their scanners searching all around them to find some clue as to why there are only fifteen ships in that system.

I check the drone's sensors again to see how the battle is going and I'm shocked at what I see. The fact that the defense system is working fine and taking care of the enemy ships is not the problem, it's that the ships are barely fighting back and one of the larger ships is heading away from the battle and no one is taking notice. Suddenly a ship from the planet is making its way toward the large ship. I send the drone on its fastest speed toward the lone enemy ship and attach it to the hull as soon as possible so as not to lose it.

The ship from the planet is actually a shuttle and it docks with the enemy warship for five minutes before it leaves again. I take those five minutes to switch the drone to the shuttle instead of the ship.

"Admiral, I have contact about ten minutes away from the system, and I count eighty-seven markers on the screen."

I'm not sure who spoke because I don't recognize the voice but this information is scary. I have a thought and if it proves true will piss off my friend royally.

"Are the eighty-seven ships stationary by any chance?"

"They are Admiral. What do you want me to do?"

"Nothing at the moment, just keep them in sensor range. All ships to their position and await further orders."

I cut the comm and switch to Weil in the next system. The Brandari system is barely an hour away and I will need the sixth fleet if we want to stand a chance against a group that large.

"Weil, any movement on your end yet?"

"Nothing Admiral. It is strange as I would think we would be a tempting target for an attack, not that I mind actually."

"You are a target, just not yet. I can't explain yet but you will not receive a force in your system if you can bring your fleet to these coordinates."

I send the coordinates to Weil's ship and come back on the comm.

"I need you to hurry as this might determine the fate of the Alliance more than any other attack."

"On our way Admiral. I'll send a message to the council."

Soon all the ships from Diana's fleet have assembled at the coordinates given and there's nothing to do but wait for Weil. Before I talk to Diana, I need hard evidence of what my suspicions are. I go back to the drone and set it to capture the vibrations and transfer them to language. I also record everything it hears just to make sure.

"Prime General I assure you that we had no idea of the fleet coming to our system to help. We never asked for it that is for sure."

"That mistake cost us fourteen ships Councilor. You and your system will pay for the damage done to them. The price for your failure to honor the agreement."

"Now wait a minute there Prime General. We agreed to be a staging point for your military in exchange for protection and a profit of the pillage you will be doing. We sent that fleet away and it was your decision to sacrifice fourteen of your oldest ships to make a show of invasion. You will not pin these costs on us."

"Or what Councilor, you will destroy me? I have more ships

in the home system then all the ships combined in the Alliance, and that is not counting all the other systems we control. I can crush you anytime I want."

He stops talking and seems to walk away a bit until he turns back and anger in his voice is evident.

"What is the meaning of this treachery?" he screams.

"What are you talking about, what treachery?"

"Not only is my fleet being watched by the same ships that were here not too long ago and you told me they had left, but I've received word from all but two of my fleets sent to subjugate this Alliance and all have been destroyed, down to the last ship!"

Two fleets, which means Rockwall and another. Earth or Conra? Conra is protected but Earth is just too far away from any of my fleets to make the trip in time. I feel sick, even if I'm not from Earth, or Human for that matter, that planet cannot fall or it would mean the end of the Alliance.

"That cannot be, no one has that kind of fleet. The only ones that have enough ships to protect one system are the Corps, and there is no way they would work together."

I have the drone detach in the entry of the planet so it gets destroyed in the atmosphere and no one detects it. I need to advise Diana that they are blown and to watch themselves.

"Diana, what's your status?"

"We've been detected by the large fleet but they still haven't move. One of their ships was on patrol and came close to us. The second it detected us it went straight back to the fleet."

"I know I heard it straight from the mouth of the Prime General."

"The what?"

"Prime General. That's the name of their military leader

I believe. Either they have translators or they speak perfect English. I still do not know what they are called. The PG said they have more ships back at their home system and in others, many times what they sent here. Oh, and he also found out that his other fleets have been destroyed, all except the one in Rockwall that is currently being contested and another one. Not sure if the target is Earth or Conra V."

"How did you hear that Prime General talking? Who was he talking to?"

"One of the Councilors from the surface."

There, it is said. I hate what will happen next.

"Those mother fucking sons of whores…" Diana screams before realizing she was on the bridge of a warship and was in charge.

"Wow, didn't expect that at all. I knew you would be pissed, but you're always so nice and proper."

"I left that planet because of all the power-hungry politicians ruining the lives of the general populace. That's it, their dead."

"All in good time Diana. First, we need to take care of that fleet. Weil should be at their location in about twenty minutes. Prepare your fleet to advance on them and make sure you arrive about three or four minutes before Weil so the enemy is concentrated on you and Weil can then surprise them. I'll let you know when they get in sensor range of the enemy. At that point fire every weapon you have in one volley. That should attract their attention."

"And after we've kicked their asses, I'm going down there and executing every last Councilor in that round shit hole."

"You won't be alone Commodore Diana, the whole crew of every ship still alive will go with you." Says the Captain from earlier.

Unknown to Diana I had included all her Captains in the conversation, so they heard the outburst at hearing the treachery of her people and the hate in her voice. At that point she won the whole fleet, cause I'm sure by the time they get to battle with the large fleet every person on all twenty-five ships will have heard the conversation in part or in whole.

At the right moment Diana's fleet jump out of their staging area and head for the fleet that at this moment must think them crazy for attacking them. I'm counting on them to monitor us and hopefully take a twenty-five-ship fleet seriously enough not to look for another one coming behind them. That reminds me of what Stephanie did a few minutes ago. I contact Weil and tell them to shut down their IFF.

Almost right away I lose all twenty-five ships from my conscience and any chance the enemy fleet has of noticing them fades to barely above zero. The only way to spot them would be a spotter close to where they pass.

Now I have to wait and observe what rage can do to motivate a fleet.

"Diana, you should have your fleet slow down a bit so you get there only a minutes before Weil. With their IFF off, the enemy won't see them coming."

"Sorry Admiral, no can do. Our jump settings for some reason are set to max or stop. I can't change them."

Of course, that's bullshit, but it's her way of letting me and the rest of the ships know that she's pissed and hopes they are as well because they'll be alone for five minutes with eighty-seven ships.

"Understood Commodore. Please have it repaired before your next fight please. I wouldn't want you to get in trouble for something as stupid as a faulty jump setting."

My way of telling the fleet that I understand but it better not happen again. I get a few thank you from some of the captains but nothing else. They are already in battle mode and they'll need all their concentration if they wish to survive.

I wish I had another drone in the Kroh system but looks like I'm stuck watching what my soldiers do with those five minutes. I make sure the five minutes will be recorded, either to show everyone what never to do or what can be done when your motivation is at its best. Thirty seconds to normal space the fleet does a course correction and come out of jump at a completely different point than originally planned, which probably saved their lives as a group of twenty large warships fire at the time and location the fleet was supposed to come out. They come out only a few thousand kilometers away at a different jump point with engines screaming full and weapons firing on closer ships.

They arrive in normal space close to the sixty-seven ships that stayed behind on the failed ambush. None of them are expecting the enemy fleet to come from there so their shields are down and none have weapons hot. Blasters, Gauss rounds and missiles hit bulkhead instead of shield and the damage is scary. Several of the ships simply blow up while others try evasive maneuvers but far too late and they also receive crippling damage. By the time most of the surviving ships have gotten their shields up and are ready to counter this surprise they have lost sixteen ships to this first attack.

Diana has her fleet spread out and continue to pound the enemy with all their weapons and leave nothing to chance. She instructs them to gang up on one ship, three per ship, and take it out before going to the next. This leaves them open to retaliation but none of them seem to care. Suddenly dozens of small icons appear on the sensors and I remember that Diana has a platoon of fighters among her ships, and they seem as pissed as their commander because they speed away toward the twenty ships that tried to ambush them. Do they really think that three dozen fighters can take down twenty large warships? The answer normally would be no but don't tell the pilots that, because they won't believe you.

I then notice a warning line of data in my mind and finally see how thirty-six fighters can expect to destroy the warships. They are carrying four full nuclear warheads each. That makes seven nuclear warheads per warship.

The Alliance has banned nuclear warheads all across its territory with reason, but this system has no life at all so the fallout is minimal and the option of letting the enemy win is not acceptable. I check the time and the fighters will have plenty of time to fire their payload before Weil gets here, but the Brandari will still detect the fallout. I just hope it doesn't create tension in the fleets.

The large enemy warships approach the fighters like they have everything else, with confidence. This enemy will soon learn of their mistake. Once their head honchos back on their home planet discovers that none of their ships have survived, they will investigate and soon find that Humans and their allies in the Alliance are ruthless fighters and innovative in their fighting style. The next large war will be much different than this one. As soon as the fighters get in range of the warships' weapons they put on more speed and scatter all over the place making it difficult for gunners to take them out. Once they approach the ships enough, they let go of their payload and storm out of there. At first, I think the warheads are duds and this was all for nothing but then as the first one explodes, I realize they were on a timer to make sure the pilots had time to distance themselves from the shock and radiation.

Anyone not behind sensors like me, or a view screen like all bridge crews and looking at those twenty warships, are now blind forever. The energy radiating from those blasts is such that it might affect the jump points in the whole system. But after the energy dissipates there is nothing left in that section, just space dust if at all.

After the initial shock of the blast the enemy warships left in the fight don't have much fight into them and send out a cease fire request and their surrender. I have all communications blocked before the images of this fight come out and delete all recordings that the mainframe back home has.

The enemy powers down their weapons and lower their shields and I quickly send a message to all Captains to accept the surrender and not fire.

Out of twenty-five ships coming in against eighty-seven, Diana lost only one ship. The enemy lost all but fourteen ships, and those are badly damaged. We will have to collect all destroyed ships so we can rebuild those fourteen and add them to our fleets. None of our ships are equipped with a containment cell large enough for all crew still alive on those fourteen ships, but just then Weil arrives and that fleet has a few ships with large cargo holds that will do just fine.

"Weil, please secure the ships and crew and tow the ships and the wrecks back to Conra V. Diana still has an unfinished job back home."

"Will do Admiral. What do I tell my crews about the radiation?"

Of course, Weil must mention it, it is in the nature of all Brandari to make sure all lives are safe.

"Tell them that we are in desperate times and to stay clear of that section if possible."

"Yes Admiral."

"Weil, are you good with this?"

"Taking care of the prisoners yes, the use of nuclear weapons no."

"When you get home, I'll have a project for you. I'll hook you up with Augustine my tech, she'll be able to help you with anything you'll need."

"Yes Admiral."

The connection cuts and I can already see Weil's fleet sending marines to the ships while technicians are preparing the ships and wrecks for transport. I switch back to Diana.

"You my friend have made someone seriously pissed."

"Let me guess, Weil? She's never liked nuclear weapons and I expected her to be pissed off. She'll get over it."

"She? I thought Brandari did not have a gender?"

"They don't but Weil always said she associates more with the female side of Humans than the male side, so she told us to consider her a woman for easier conversation."

"Now you tell me, after so many weeks!"

"I thought she would have mentioned it herself. Admiral, I've got to get back to Kroh to capture that Prime General and to do a little cleaning on the council."

"I know. Prep a small drone I can use to follow you and the rest to the surface. I need to record the events in case the Alliance comes calling."

Diana's fleet thank Weil and her fleet and they head back to Kroh. They get there just as the shuttle is on final approach to the last warship in the system. Right away the defense system protects the warship so Diana orders her ships to take it out

214

and she takes four ships to intercept the enemy ship. They get there just in time and take out its engines and then surround it and order it to surrender.

"You Human scum will not be able to stop the Donderi. We will crush you and kill every last one of you..."

Diana has her Captain fire several blaster shots at points on the ship that are heavily armored so the ship shakes but no real damage occurs.

"Prime General, I swear to you right now that I will personally kill you if you don't shut up. I will have marines come aboard your ship and escort you to the surface on that shuttle you just arrived in. More marines will accept the surrender of your crew. If any of them even looks at them funny they will have orders to execute that person as well as another one, just as a message. Do you understand me?"

"How do you know my title?"

"Do you understand me?" she yells again.

"I do."

Diana cuts the comm and switches back to me.

"Admiral, how do you suggest I proceed on the surface?"

"This is your home world Diana, your call. Please leave the captains on the ships in case another wave comes in system. You can take whoever and as many as you feel you will need."

"Excellent, I will go alone and bring your drone."

With that she cuts the connection and walks to the bay. She takes one of the attack shuttles and despite her desire to do this alone a squad of ten marines come aboard and ignore her orders to get off. One of the marines takes command of the shuttle and they leave, Diana left to sit down and accept their help.

They arrive on the surface and a full platoon of Kroh soldiers wait for her arrival with guns pointed at the shuttle. Diana looks each of the marines in the eye and simply tells them to follow her lead. She opens the hatch and simply walks off the shuttle, looking at the platoon who raise their weapons, and strolls toward the council chamber which is a ten-minute walk from the spaceport. The marines walk behind her, hands on their weapons and looking all around. The small group attracts a lot of attention and not all of it good but the only person that tries to cut her off she takes her blaster out and shoots him in the head. She whispers that this was an aide to one of the worse Councilors on the planet. No one else tries to stop them until they get to the council chambers and a row of guards stand in their way. The marines walk past Diana and form a row in front of her.

Diana and the lead guard look at each other with the intensity I know when Diana is talking telepathically and after a long conversation the lead guard orders his men to fall in line and leads Diana and the marines into the chambers. When Diana breaks down the large wooden doors of the main chamber the Councilors startle and ask the lead guard what the meaning of this interruption is.

Diana shoots that man in the head as well as four others. None of the guards move to stop her. After the commotion stops, she takes the podium and addresses the crowd.

"The five stronger Councilors, and the most corrupt are dead. I know all of you are far from clean, but your crimes are much lesser and can be overlooked for now. Councilor Germaine Fortier had brokered a deal with the Donderi, an enemy of the Alliance and I know that the other four dead Councilors had a large part in it as well. This deal is now over and all Donderi forces here and elsewhere have been defeated by my employer Admiral Sherry-Ann Lebronski. As of now, The Red Widow Group will take control of protecting this system, with me as the commander of the fleet, and no more treachery will be accepted. Do I make myself clear?"

No one answered but a few nodded.

"I need an answer now people or I continue executing people!"

"Understood." All say as one.

"Captain, I leave you with the removal of the traitors and I want you to let me know of all transgressions by anyone of the council or of the ones that will replace the traitors."

"Yes Commodore Gnalls!"

And with that the soldiers started their job and Diana left.

18

Chapter 18

"Hey Brenda, how close are you to Rockwall?" I ask.

"Three minutes out, why?"

"Just before a minute out have all your ships shut down their IFF. The enemy won't know you're coming."

"Neither will Aunt Martha."

"She'll know soon enough and the surprise will outweigh the negatives trust me."

"Alright they're off. Martha told me they had fifty-two ships in their fleet. All ships are at port since they're scheduled to leave tomorrow for protection runs for the ten transports to various planets. If not for that, they would have faced the one hundred twenty-five ships with barely a dozen ships."

"Even with your fleet, do you think you can defeat them? The Widow's fleets have done great so far but I have no clue as to Aunt Martha's crews."

"Well, every ship's Captain wishes he would be hired by Hector Corp so they can become one of Aunt Martha's sons or daughters. Before you came along Admiral if a job opening came up in her unit, she would have thousands of applicants a minute after posting it. No one wanted another unit if they could. Now, there are two units the people want to be in."

"How's her boss?"

"He's a fairly decent guy from what I heard."

"That's good to know."

They're about one minute to jump back to normal space so their IFF come off and I lose the whole group for a full minute. I look up the information on Alain Hector and his companies. Unlike my ex, Hector did not branch out in dozens of domains trying to make a quick buck here and there. He started his company by making armor plating for shuttles and soon became known for the great quality of his products and service, so he grew his company to make plating for ships and freighters. Soon after that he purchased a few local companies making electronics, framing, engines and even weapons. All were local companies and the old owners were glad to sell to him as he always kept the companies local. All five companies have grown exponentially since their beginning and now Hector Corp is one of the best manufacturers of freighters and shuttles in the Alliance.

This might be a good decision that Brenda took as it might give me an opening to grow the friendship circle the Group has.

The fleet open their IFF, arrives behind the Donderi and blast their engines to max to try and lend a hand as soon as possible. From the sensors Aunt Martha is holding her own but it's clear they are in over their heads. Then Brenda and her fleet open up at maximum range with Gauss rifles and blasters. Missiles are useless right now as they will be shot down before they get to their destination as they take too much time to get there. Closer to the targets will give them a better chance of hitting the Donderi.

The Gauss rounds are sent concentrated on just a few targets for maximum effect and it pays off as eight ships disappear behind large explosions of the engine bays. The blasters are sent at several other ships to take some of the heat off Martha and it works as fifty of the remaining ships turn to face them. That might have worked much better than expected because now they are outnumbered severely, but Aunt Martha is not one to be overshadowed so she sends ten of her larger ships to the side and to repeat Brenda's strategy. Much closer than the Widows were, Martha's ships send barrage after barrage of missiles, Gauss rounds and blasters at the fifty ships. Another five of the fifty follow their fellow ships into oblivion while the forty-five other ships seem to hesitate as to who to attack.

Well, the defenders and back up do not hesitate and attack. Brenda, now close enough to fire everything does so and the sensors become a solid wall of missiles, Gauss rounds and blaster bolts toward the enemy while Aunt Martha's ships to the same. A few of the Donderi ships fire back but they all seem confused. The ten defender ships must have destroyed the leader of the group in their initial attack and now the ships find themselves with no one to give orders or too many doing so.

Both groups spend ammo after ammo without stopping. I take a moment to look at the rest of the Donderi attacking Aunt Martha's lead group and the success of the other group seem to have given them energy because all of a sudden, all forty ships left spring forth and close the distance with the enemy and just let them have it all.

The fighting looks more like a street brawl than a space battle, but soon none of the Donderi ships are a threat and every one of my ships, the twenty-three left, keep guard on the enemy while Aunt Martha picks up the crew members that have survived the space battle but have no way to get planet side.

A comm comes in from the lead ship to Brenda's ship.

"Commodore Vixon, we owe you our lives." Aunt Martha says.

"Nonsense Aunt Martha, you guys were doing great, we just distracted them enough for you to finish the job."

That's crap and Brenda knows it, but when dealing with an Admiral of the renown of Aunt Martha, always best to downplay your role.

"That's crap Brenda. We were barely holding and that only because my crews are the best. You guys are excellent and work great together and with others. I would not mind having your fleet in my employ."

"That is incredible praise Martha, but our current employer is pretty much as incredible as you are and I don't think anyone on my crew would switch employers."

"No one has ever refused one of my offers. That man must be incredible if you want to stay with him."

"Her actually Admiral." I say.

"And to whom am I talking to now?"

"Admiral Sherry-Ann Lebronski of The Red Widow Group. I must say it is a pleasure talking to such a woman as you Aunt Martha."

"Lebronski, aren't you the one that saved Fernon a few weeks back? That was some light show you put on Sherry. I can call you Sherry, can I?"

"All my friends do and I sincerely hope you will become one of them."

"I need to ask you a serious question Sherry and I want an honest answer. If you wish to talk privately, I will understand."

"Go ahead Martha, I have nothing to hide from any of my people."

"Why did you come help us? What's the end game if there is one?"

"Actually, Martha you'll have to thank Brenda for that. I found out you were in trouble and she was heading here five minutes before she arrived. As for an end game, I had none but after looking at your employer's business, I believe we can become trade partners and continue to help each other in the future. The Donderi are not finish with us I'm sorry to say. All the friends we can make to defeat them will be welcome."

"Well Sherry, I would love to thank both you and Brenda planet side. Will you join her?"

"I'd love to if I were there in person, but I'm still back on Conra V and we have our own infection of vermin at the moment."

"How the hell can we talk live if you're on Conra V. Then again, how are you not dead with the poison on the surface?"

"Your first question is hard to explain but leave it at Conranian tech. As for the second question, the planet is now perfectly safe, with green fields and lush fruit trees. You can come at any time Martha. I'll make sure that your ships are all on the safe list for safe passage to the planet."

"Can I even ask how you healed the planet?"

"I'm not even sure myself. All I know is the power that's inside me was able to heal the planet. I'm not sure I even want to know how."

"I agree. Well as soon as we've healed a bit and given your people one of the best party they'll ever have I will send them back to you and will follow them with my ship. I might ask Alain to join me. Seems he might like to be one of the first businessman to broker a deal with Conra V."

19

Chapter 19

I finally get out of the system, my brain hurting like I was run over by a shuttle, and find a few of Ben's men preparing some medical equipment. I barely move, just turning my head slightly so as not to make noise and just watch them working. I'm not sure what they are doing but it is clear they have orders because every person has a purpose and none get in the way of the others.

One of my fingers brushes against something on the seat I'm lying in and that object falls to the ground making every battle harden soldier jump like scared kids. It's too hard to stop myself and I burst out laughing.

"I'm sorry I scared you guys. I was admiring the way you all work together, it is fascinating. Now what's all this for?"

"You Admiral. We had orders from Brenda to prepare all medical equipment to revive you in case you had a problem."

"How long have I been out?"

"About six hours Admiral."

"That's it? It felt like days in there."

"Now you know how I feel Admiral." Brenda butts in.

"Thank you, gentlemen, it seems we won't need that equipment this time, but leave it here for the future."

The soldiers leave and I'm left alone, except for Brenda, who now that we're alone talks to me inside my head.

'I've never seen anyone work this system like you did, let alone survive it.'

'Thank you, Brenda. Now, how are we here? Any sign of the Donderi?'

'So that's their race. Then this is bad news but we can talk about that later. We have an armada of a hundred ships heading our way.'

'Any of our other fleets close enough to help?'

'None. Most are still at their designated location. I believe that was your doing?'

'Yes, I want to make sure all our friends are well protected.'

'Won't be any good if we're dead now, will it?'

'Is an AI supposed to have sarcasm in their subroutines?'

'No, it's a result of years working with Humans mainly. Not many of the old Conranians had much emotion. Now, for the armada. The defense system is able to defeat a fleet of up to thirty to thirty-five depending on the configuration. With the system and twelve ships, are chances are not that great.'

'Don't forget we have a crazy Conranian with great power.'

'That she cannot use in space unless she has learned of a way to breath in vacuum.'

'Working on it. Alright let's go top side and see what we can do. You have control of the defense system Brenda?'

'What else would I be doing at a moment like this?'

'You've got an attitude problem little lady. Keep it, I love it.' I say as I run down the corridor to the surface.

I arrive at the control room where Ben has set up shop and

has his people working and learning the controls. With no force menacing the surface of the planet, he sent most of his forces with the *Hand of God* so they can prepare a boarding of several of the Donderi ships. His second in command has leadership of the marines while he keeps control of the army on the surface. Before saying anything, I look at how the men and women under his directions going from one screen to the other trying to predict where the Donderi will jump in system but he seems to be having trouble with something.

"I'm telling you sir, they either have a cloaking device or some sort of jammer because I can't pinpoint their exact entry point." The tech says.

"That's because they're coming from multiple points. They're learning from us. Ben, would you happen to have a spare headset?"

He hands me one that has Admiral written on the head ban.

"It's the most comfortable one." Ben says as way of explaining. What a gentleman.

"Attention home fleet, we've got a hundred ships coming in but I can tell you that for the last six hours I've watched the rest of the fleet kick ass with these Donderi pricks. Here's the points of entry and the numbers associated to them. I've given the points names for easy comprehension. Alpha has eight ships coming in. Bravo has twenty coming. Charlie will see forty-six, Delta with twenty and Echo with six will seal the deal. You know your crews best, where do you think you'll be most effective?"

"I've got Alpha." Says Helen Greaves of the *Angry Grandpa*.

"I'll go along with her…" starts to say one of the other Captains but Helen cuts him off.

"No, I said I've got Alpha. You guys take care of the rest.

Brenda, if you could spare two attack drones to keep the ships centered on me there?"

"Will do Captain Greaves." Brenda replies.

"Are you sure about this Helen?" I ask her.

"It's time your newer faster ships see what a real ship can do." She says with pride in her voice.

"Alright then, Alpha's taken care of. What's next?"

"Brent and I could probably take Echo alone. What do you think buddy?" Hector Trenton of the *Flying Castle* asks Brent Deveraux of the *Silver Knight*.

"Damn right Hector. My pilots will be happy to stretch out their wings and kick some ass."

"We'll go with the group that hits Charlie." Says Paul of the *Hand of God*. "With forty-six ships, my marines will have better chances of boarding one of them and taking control."

"I'll join him there as well." Says Elena of my *Red Widow*.

"I can take *Longbow* and *Shadow Ghost* at both Bravo and Delta." Says Brenda. "I'll have two of the moon's each as well as three attack drones each. If Madison and Benny don't mind of course."

"I'll be honored miss Brenda." Says Madison.

"Same here sweet cheeks." Says Benny.

"And how do you know their sweet Benny? Unlike you, I've seen what you look like, all of you."

"And, the verdict?" asks Benny.

"Maybe I should work on getting myself a body. What do you think Admiral?"

"I am not getting into this discussion with you guys."

"The rest of you will join Elena and Paul at Charlie. I don't like it, only one Gauss rifle between the seven of you. I've noticed that it's the most effective against the Donderi."

227

"Admiral, I might have a solution for you. How comfortable do you think you are with the mind control of the system?"

"Very by now, why?"

"We have ten minutes before the Donderi arrive in system, so everyone take your places and I'll check if we can get you some more help." Says Brenda.

I can see every ship moving to their designated jump points and Brenda invades my mind again.

'I'm not invading your mind, just talking to you and reading your most personal thoughts.'

'That's called invading miss AI.'

We head out of the control center and now I feel naked because I can't even tell what the fleet is doing.

'Don't worry Sherry, if what I'm thinking works, you'll be connected to all ships I've got a tracker on just like me. It will put a strain on your brain, but I'll show you how to control it and how to block it if need be.'

'That will be great Brenda. After getting a taste of all that information at the tip of my mind and now being blind...'

'That's what it felt like when the Vuldalians bombed the planet and destroyed all the relay stations in the system. It took me a full century to rebuild the stations and the defense system.'

'How exactly did you repair them?'

'I have access to a small repair bay on one of the moons that was able to repair the attack drones first and then I used the drones to repair the moons and the station.'

I walk into a small building that's basically just a reinforced elevator shaft. I head down to the lowest level where I can't even hear the army's vehicles driving noisily on top. The doors open and I find myself in a small dressing room I guess, as it has a comfortable bench and a locker in front of it. Brenda at that moment stays silent so I walk to the locker and open it to find what I can only guess is a space suit, but a slim one made for a woman. I grab the helmet for the suit and see a name on it.

Zoe Brookes, my ancestor.

Can it be? Did she wear this suit to whatever end Brenda has in store for me?

'Yes, she did Sherry. Zoe was not able to operate the system you did earlier but if I blocked that part of the helmet, she was able to pilot the ship behind the glass.'

I turn around as light come on the other side of the said glass to find a ship, small like Chicago's ship but sleek and menacing. This ship looks dangerous just sitting there.

'Is this what you meant by giving the home fleet help?'

'It is Sherry. You're going to pilot it into battle and help where needed.'

'News flash Brenda, I don't know the first thing about piloting a ship, or anything else on a ship.'

'Relax, the system will tell you how. Put the suit on and grab the helmet. Once you come close to the ship it will open for you and you can get settled in the seat.'

'How many crew members does it have?'

'None, just you.'

I walk into the chamber the ship rests in and slowly walk around it to look at what I guess is my personal ship. It's small enough that it will fit easily in the *Red Widow*'s bay so I can bring her anywhere I go. I approach it a bit more to touch it and an opening form before my eyes. What kind of hatch is this with no inner hatch in case there is vacuum on the other side, or poisonous air?

I walk inside and soon find the pilot's seat but it's reclined so much I'm not sure I'll be able to see anything in front of the ship.

'You won't have to Sherry. Just sit down and place the helmet on your head.'

I walk to the seat and do as Brenda asks and the second the helmet touches the rest of the suit it seals itself and data assaults my mind the same way it did earlier today. I work at it the same way I did in the initial moments of that connection and the data eases and my mind relaxes. Unlike Zoe, I want the information on my fleet at the moment so I let it flow inside me but place to the side the data from every fleet except the one in the home system. I can also access the data on the moons and the drones.

All of a sudden, instructions flood my mind about how to fly this ship, use weapons, jump drive and all other ship systems. As this information is inputted inside my mind, I check up on the rest of the home fleet and find the Donderi just coming in system at all five jump points at the same time.

At alpha point the *Angry Grandpa* doesn't even move away from the eight ships coming fast at him. All eight Donderi ships fire at the huge ship in front of them but the shields hold. One of the ships goes to veer off to fly past the ship but a super-fast drone fires at it hard enough that the ship comes back into the formation which coincides with Helen ordering all weapons free, and the space around jump point alpha lights up.

The four forward Gauss rifles fire at two ships creating a major hole in the shields of those ships with gives the thirty forward heavy blasters free reign to the haul and they do serious damage to it. Both ships are now open to vacuum and are not responsive. The thirty missiles fired hit another pair of ships which creates again a hole in the shields which a second round of four Gauss rounds hit right into the hauls and vaporize the ship up to the engine rooms. Both disappear in impressive fireballs.

Not even a minute into the fight and Helen's crew has destroyed half her opponents. Too bad we don't have more ships like him, because I would place one at every jump point. The four ships try to punch for speed to evade the large warship but the drones do exactly what they are here for and hit the ships leaving too far off the arc of attack the *Angry Grandpa* has. Helen has her gunners fire a round of Gauss rifle on each ship as well as five missiles and five blasters each. The ten missiles left in the tubes fire a few seconds later at a single opponent.

When the first wave hits the ships, one explodes on impact while the rest have severe damage all over. The second wave of missiles hits the single ship and are supplemented by the ten blasters not fired. That ship follows his brothers and dies spectacularly.

Despite the drone's best efforts, the last two ships make it past the *Angry Grandpa* and move to intercept but Helen calls them off and doesn't even turn her ship after them, she just fires the two Gauss rifles, six missile tubes and fifteen blasters at the two retreating ships. The supersonic rounds of the Gauss rifles hit the back shields and continue on to the ship, destroying the engines. The blasters hit the ships and making sure the engines are never repaired and finally the missiles hit what's left of the ships and two more explosions light up the space around the huge warship.

Helen finally turns her ship around and heads for the planet to be the last line of defense, hopefully arriving on time to prevent anyone ground side from getting hurt.

The battle at alpha took so little time that I still have not assimilated all the information about my new ship. If anyone after today bothers Helen about her old ship it's because their idiots. I save all the footage and data to the server so I can send it to all Widow ships. Helen has now passed from laughing stock to heroine.

"Whoa Helen, leave some action for us, will you?" says Elena, leader of the home fleet. She understands what just happens and is sure that all other ships understand it also.

"Just don't let any of them get through you or they're ours. The old man still has plenty of ammo and we're not even breaking a sweat."

I open a channel just to Helen.

"Helen, are you able to change course slightly so you'll be in rifle range for Charlie point?"

"I can do that Admiral. You don't want the ships there to take care of it by themselves?"

"Forty-six against seven are far from great odds, even if we do have the best crews. As soon as you're in range start taking down Donderi crap."

"Yes ma'am." She says with a smile in her voice.

I now switch to echo point where my two ships are alone against six opponents and don't have near as much armor as the old man. Neither of those ships is fast but they have the bonus of twenty-four fighters that can create havoc and leave the enemy open to the guns of their larger friends. Although the *Silver Knight* doesn't have much in the way of offensive weapons, the *Flying Castle* is basically a smaller version of the old man and can dish out serious damage. Now I understand why Hector suggested teaming up with Brent. While his ship has incredible firepower, Brent's fighters can create confusion that will help his gunners hitting their target. Brent will probably stay in the background as his armor and weapons are not the best, but his smaller friends are there to do the work.

"Brent brother, I need you to coordinate. I'm gonna have my hands full trying to shoot down the large ships while not hitting our smaller friends, so I need you to point out the best targets and my gunners will follow your finger. We got this my friend."

And just like that Hector gave Brent one of the most important jobs of the battle so he can feel included.

The information on flying my ship is now complete and I start the pre-flight checklist to make sure it's in fighting shape after so many centuries of inaction.

'Brenda, what's the name of this ship by the way?'

'*Killer Queen*. It was given its name because it was expected that Zoe become queen one day and she was ruthless with this ship.'

'Let's hope I can live up to her name.'

The fighters swarm the Donderi ships and evade the rapid fire of the anti-fighter weaponry. Then Brent starts his targeting procedure.

"Gunners, second on your left, that huge mother fucker, give it all you have."

Three Gauss rifles, twelve missiles and twenty large blasters fire at the ship. Brent was right in that it was huge, close to the size of the *Flying Castle*. Targeting it first with everything was good thinking as it freed the fighters to harass the smaller ships, the ones they had a chance to take down. The weaponry fires as soon as Brent gives the order and as the missile explosions subside only black nothingness is left between the two other ships next to it.

The fighters are now swarming mostly around a single ship, the smallest of the group and Brent sees one of its brother ships coming for a rescue.

"The ship heading to help the smaller one, two Gauss and ten blasters. The ships on the right of the smaller one the rest of the weapons."

The gunners fire where directed and both ships join their larger friend. Then the shields on the *Flying Castle* give way and it takes damage from the two remaining Donderi ships.

"Hector, take control I'll go help my fighters."

"Got it my friend, nice targeting."

Brent has his engines to full, which is not saying much as it's barely faster than the *Angry Grandpa* but the target is close by and he has his fighters leave the ship alone for a few seconds as two missiles and five large blasters hit it. The ship shakes and shows signs of serious damage as the fighters swarm back in and soon have to fly away at top speed as the enemy ship's engine overheat. Brent turns the ship sideways so the fighters can all hide behind its side and as the ship explodes the larger pieces hit the shields of the *Silver Knight* instead of the vulnerable fighters.

Hector is in a death match with the two Donderi ships and Brent decides to lend a hand. He fires his meager two missiles and five large blasters again at the ship that looks the most damaged and barely seems to do anything. A few seconds later a single Gauss rifle hits the same ship and it explodes as the engines simply lose all their fuel in an instant.

The *Flying Castle* fires everything else at the other ship and it suddenly simply stops doing anything and power comes off.

The floating wreck will need investigating later, but Brent asks a squad of fighters to stay close by in case it's some kind of ruse.

I look at what the *Flying Castle*'s computer tells me of the damage it sustained during the fight and it is severe. Hector lost some good people today which means I lost some good people. I will have to make a ceremony on Conra V for all those lost in the service of the Alliance and I'll invite the President to see how many people sacrificed their lives for the protection of his citizens. My goal is not political but if it pushes him to raise the budget on defense then all the better.

The *Killer Queen* is ready to go and surprisingly in perfect condition and fully stocked. I suspect Brenda has something to do with this. I give the command for the large doors at the end of a long launching pad to open and push the ship to its max so I can join the fight and help my people. I hate the fact that all of them have placed themselves in danger while I stayed nice and cozy in a secure location. No more of that.

The speed is phenomenal and in no time, I come out of Conra V's atmosphere and head for Charlie jump point.

"Back up is coming ladies and gentlemen."

"Admiral, is that you in that little ship?"

The seven ships at Charlie point are locked in battle and taking serious damage so before answering I fly past them at incredible speed and fire all I have at the same time. The *Queen* only has two Gauss rifles and six forward large blasters, but combined with the speed and incredible armor and shields, it is devastating on the battlefield. Both Gauss rounds hit one ship and actually go right through and hit another behind it enough to take down the shields temporarily so I fire my six blasters at that one and open it to vacuum, although the ship is still functional. That doesn't last though as Elena has the *Widow* fire its single Gauss rifle right at the same place I opened and the round finishes the job.

With this simple act the Widow ships have new energy and start hitting the Donderi ships hard. They had taken out four ships before I got here so there are still forty left, but they seem hesitant suddenly. I take a second to look at bravo and delta jump points and the battle is fierce but in good hands. I think of something devious and ask Brenda if she's free while I fire all my weapons at a smaller ship and destroy it.

'I'm always free Admiral. What do you have in mind?'

'Choose one of the ships at Charlie, not the one the marines are on, and send one of your trackers on it.'

'So, we can let it leave and see where their home planet is?'

'You read my mind.'

'Sorry, I invaded your mind again.'

'You are forgiven.'

Another ship follows all its brothers into hell from concentrated fire of my ships and I start going after the smaller ones while the big ones I leave to my ships. Another four ships go down when the *Ray of Light* comes apart and explodes. Now I'm pissed.

Before I can do anything about it three ships on my right and two on my left explode in spectacular fashion, exactly like...

The *Angry Grandpa* and *Flying Castle* have joined the fight and they seem as pissed as I am. A message over the Widow frequency sounds music to my ears.

"We have control of the ship."

The marines start a rampage in the back of the group of Donderi ships and Brenda sends a message to all ships not to hit a certain ship. The now formidable Widow force at

Charlie jump point pound everything they have, and I simply go from one position to another either finishing damaged ships or taking out shields for others to finish off. In less than two minutes after the takeover of the Donderi ship they are starting their retreat but the Widow ships are on them something bad. To make sure the decoy ship does not cause suspicion I hit it with a single Gauss round to take out the shields and fire a couple of blasters to none essential section and let it go after as I go after bigger fish.

The decoy ship jumps and we finish the rest of the ships except two more that also get away. I look at bravo and delta and both are now quiet. Three more ships got away with a total of six. If my calculations are correct, and being inside a computer helps being right, out of five hundred eighty-five ships sent to destroy the Alliance, only six escaped. Not a bad count.

"Will anyone be able to look for possible survivors of the *Ray of Light*?"

"I'll do it." Says Elena.

"Thank you, Elena." I now plug in all the fleets for my next part. "The rest, if you're in fairly good shape, please bring the wrecks of all Donderi ships to a place Brenda will give you. We'll try and salvage some of them so we can bring our numbers back to what they were before all the attacks. We lost one ship here but several more at other locations. Thank you all for your brave work.

I'd love to say that this battle will end hostilities between the Alliance and the Donderi, but I'm afraid this was only an appetizer of what's to come. For now, let's breathe, take a few days off and then get all of your families here so we can protect them better. Thanks to the brave marines, and Rjoart, we still have twelve ships here and captured more in other systems but we now know that even with the defense system, twelve ships is far from enough.

We'll recruit as many people as we need, build ships and make sure the Alliance understands what all of you did today. All lost today will have an official funeral on Conra V and will be buried at a new cemetery we will build for members of The Red Widow Group and their families. That place will be sacred grounds from now on. All of you are heroes."

With that I fall silent and ask the ship to bring me home. I fall into myself thinking of the last few months. I started out as basically a slave and now I control the largest armada of warships in the Alliance and might be its only salvation. I have no clue how I will be able to do that alone. But I'm not alone, I have my new family with me, a very large and powerful family. I have The Red Widow Group.

The fight continues in book two, The New Alliance.

Visit ddorebooks.com for more books and series information.

Lightning Source UK Ltd.
Milton Keynes UK
UKHW010433090223
416681UK00003B/1011